"Are you a gambler, Irish?" Mike queried softly. "I know all sorts of games to play in the dark."

"Risky games?" Gabby asked.

"They can be." His hands moved beneath her sweatshirt. "But you know what they say. It's not whether you win or lose..." His fingers skimmed over her ribcage. "It's how you play the game. How do you play the game, Irish?"

She temporized. "I've never been very good at games."

"How about follow the leader?" Mike sailed light kisses down her neck. "A simple little game where everyone plays"—his mouth covered hers briefly—"and no one loses. Or hide and seek." His thumb made a shaky foray across her nipple, his long, sensitive fingers tightening convulsively until Gabby gasped. "Irish..." He drew a shuddering breath. "You can find such nice surprises playing hide and seek."

Courtney Ryan

Courtney Ryan began writing at the age of six, when she was given her first typewriter. Although her typing hasn't improved much since then, she now enjoys "seeing my fantasies—minus spelling errors, bless my editor—come to life on the printed page." She gives credit to "a very handsome and understanding husband" who joins her in research for her romantic novels. Courtney lives with her husband and children in Utah.

Dear Reader:

Laine Allen, author of *Undercover Kisses* (#276), returns with another pair of beguiling lovers in *The Fire Within* (#304). Former nurse Cara Chandler loyally hopes to build a future on the bittersweet foundation of a lost love. Dynamo millionaire Lou Capelli dreams of finding a woman honest enough to gaze at him with love—not dollar signs—in her eyes. But the passion that melds them together just as cataclysmically tears them apart. A tender and tormenting love story . . .

Prolific Lee Williams brings us *Whispers of an Autumn Day* (#305), a playful, romantic story with just a touch of suspense. Beautiful academic Lauri Fields finds herself immediately at odds with devilishly enticing Adam Brady when he won't return some love letters written by her late grandfather. Undaunted, Lauri is willing to do whatever it takes to persuade this handsome charmer to give back what's rightfully hers. But Brady employs his own brand of seduction to teach Lauri a delightful lesson . . . What fun!

Readers love the provocative openings of Jan Mathews's romances, and in *Shady Lady* (#306), she's written another hot one. This time beautiful undercover police officer Catherine Coulton is posing as a prostitute, hoping to make a quick arrest, when aggressive Nick Samuels, also an undercover cop, comes on to her like gang busters! By blending madcap humor, gritty realism, and heart-melting romance, Jan stamps *Shady Lady* with her own distinctive style. She doesn't shy away from tough subjects—after all, her husband's a policeman—but she always touches the vulnerable core of her characters . . . and the heart of every romance reader.

It's been awhile since we've published a romance by Helen Carter, whose emotionally charged love stories have earned her wide recognition among readers. In *Tender Is the Night* (#307), hero Chris Carpenter is enthralled by heroine Toni Kendall's beauty, intelligence, and sense of fun. He's also drawn to her loving, zany family, something he's never had. But though he vows to make Toni his own, she seems determined to remain fancy free—and she may be destroying their best chance for happiness . . . Once again Helen Carter writes a complex and thoroughly satisfying story.

Here's a truly exceptional first romance by a terrific new talent—*For Love of Mike* (#308) by Courtney Ryan. Just when Gabby Cates should be flying the friendly skies to Hawaii with a brand-new husband, she's really stranded on a beach in a water-logged wedding dress with her overweight Siamese cat and tall, blond, slightly intoxicated Mike Hyatt. What's more, though she's escaped the net of marriage, she's lost her job and is about to be evicted from her home! Clearly, she needs help—and Mike's only too willing to oblige. *For Love of Mike* is wonderfully witty and delightfully unpredictable. Don't miss it!

What new romance includes a cheerleader named Olga who resembles a Nazi commandant, a couple of sidekicks called Killer and Tank, a heroine who's in big trouble because she's just paid seventeen million dollars for the *worst* football team in the league, and an original tough-guy quarterback who breaks every rule in the book? Why, the latest romance from Diana Morgan, of course! *Two in a Huddle* (#309) begins with Selena Derringer passing out in Trader O'Neill's arms. It ends with a wild football game. And what happens in the middle is loads of fun. Enjoy!

Until next month, happy reading,

Ellen Edwards

Ellen Edwards, Senior Editor
SECOND CHANCE AT LOVE
The Berkley Publishing Group
200 Madison Avenue
New York, NY 10016

P.S. Don't forget that our new SECOND CHANCE AT LOVE covers begin with the February books. Every bookseller and reviewer who has seen them loves them!

Second Chance at Love

FOR LOVE OF MIKE

COURTNEY RYAN

**A SECOND CHANCE AT LOVE
BOOK**

FOR LOVE OF MIKE

First edition published December 1985

First printing

"Second Chance at Love" and the butterfly emblem are trademarks belonging to Jove Publications, Inc.

Printed in the United States of America

Second Chance at Love books are published by
The Berkley Publishing Group
200 Madison Avenue, New York, NY 10016

Chapter

1

"QUIT HISSING AT ME," Gabby muttered darkly. "If you didn't want to get your little paws wet, you shouldn't have followed me down here."

The Siamese cat answered with a yowl instead of a meow, arching its back as another wave broke onto the shoreline. The tide was rising quickly; this time the muddy brown water stained the toes of Gabby's white satin shoes before finally receding. The threat was too much for her nervous feline to face. He bounded across the damp sand, executed a flying leap over a rotting piece of driftwood, and landed on the relative safety of a jagged boulder.

Gabby stared at the chilly blue eyes suspended in the dusky twilight. The cat returned the look, faintly contemptuous and coldly impersonal.

"You're right, Kitty," Gabby admitted sadly, her voice husky with emotion. "I'm a monster. I was never worthy of someone like Alan. I should be shot for what I did to him."

The cat licked a paw clean, then yawned in Gabby's face.

"If only he had hit me, or called me names. Do you know what he did? He thanked me for my honesty. He said, 'I appreciate your honesty, Gabrielle.' I could have killed him, you know that, Kitty?"

Kitty was curled over the gray-blue stone, fast asleep. Gabby sighed and turned away, determinedly sloshing through the foamy waves that sucked at her feet. Considering the endless fittings she had endured, her custom-made wedding dress was amazingly uncomfortable. The high neckline seemed to be slowly closing around her throat, growing higher and tighter with each step she took. The fitted waistline nipped savagely at her bare skin, restricting her labored attempts at breathing. A mud-caked demi-train completed her misery, dragging behind her through the sand like a lace-trimmed ball and chain.

Gabby stumbled in her satin heels, nearly losing her balance as another wave surged against her legs. The blisters on her feet seemed to boil inside her shoes, and she felt a morbid satisfaction. She deserved to suffer. There was no finer, more sincere or understanding man on earth than Alan DeSpain.

And six hours ago, Gabrielle Cates had left him standing at the altar.

A tremendous wall of water crashed onto the beach,

rolling toward Gabby with frightening speed. Hitching her dress up to her knees, she loped to dry sand, her leaden train slapping behind. She deserved to suffer, but she did not deserve to die. Swimming in this festive satin straitjacket would be suicidal.

Exhausted, Gabby sank weakly to her knees amid dry seaweed and tiny, glasslike pieces of shell. Enough was enough. Her feet were bleeding, her dress was ruined, and her cat had probably been swept away into the Pacific Ocean by now. All in all, the cutting edge of her guilt had been somewhat dulled.

After all, she hadn't left Alan literally standing at the altar. To be precise, he had been in the small alcove adjoining the chapel, awaiting the signal to take his place at the altar. He had not been alone. Filling the alcove to capacity were Alan's father, grandfather, younger brother, best friend, and a distant cousin, all of whom shuffled out reluctantly when Gabby made her unscheduled appearance.

Throughout her hysterical explanation, Alan had remained calm. Alan had once helped deliver a baby in a stalled elevator while Gabby had looked helplessly on, trying not to be sick. Undaunted by the fact that he was not a doctor but a corporate lawyer, Alan had proceeded as if he practiced the thing daily on his lunch hour, remaining perfectly, completely calm. Alan *always* remained calm.

Yes, he understood. No, he would not want Gabby to make a commitment to him unless she was positive it was best for both of them. Yes, he forgave her, and he thanked her for her honesty.

Honesty. Gabby pulled the devil-shoes off her feet and tossed them into the surf, letting go with a string of magnificent swear words. What was honesty? Last night there had been no question in her mind that she wanted to spend the rest of her life with Alan DeSpain. She was twenty-seven years old, a mature, intelligent adult who knew exactly what she wanted out of life. Alan DeSpain was a kind, dependable, rock-solid sort of man, that rare breed who treasured hearth and home above all else. How could she do better than a man who had already established college funds for their four prospective children and talked enthusiastically about spending their retirement years touring the country in a Winnebago? Granted, it wasn't exactly moonlight and roses, but she'd had experience of that kind once before and found it simply wasn't enough. Alan offered a future with no question marks, carefully plotted out from the Hawaiian honeymoon to the golden wedding anniversary. Tranquillity and security, and a commitment based on the deepest mutual respect. Surely this was enough to lay Gabby's childhood demons to rest.

Or so she thought.

Suppressing any traitorous pangs of regret, she had said good-bye to her unorthodox lifestyle on one of southern California's more rugged and isolated stretches of coastline. She had taken her farewell dinner of tuna sandwiches and Oreos to the beach, donating most of it to the gulls who filled the air with their demanding screams. She had stripped off her jeans and sneakers, wearing only a faded football jersey for her final swim beneath a misty half-moon. Later, she had walked through each empty room of her shabby beach house, dodging the cardboard boxes that held her few belongings. She had told herself how fortunate she was to be moving into Alan's beautiful home in Orange County, and out of this bug-infested excuse for a rental unit.

And she had believed it. Right up until the moment her best friend, Alicia, had tried to pin the veil on her gleaming, shoulder-length black hair. That one small act had released a flood of panic so intense that Gabby had known she would never become Mrs. Alan DeSpain. After she spoke to Alan, her flight from the church had been nonstop, skirts hitched to her knees, the faint sounds of organ music drifting from the chapel lending wings to her feet. She had briefly considered some sort of public apology or explanation or whatever it was one did in a situation of this sort. Certainly Aunt Helen would have insisted on it. But the feisty widow who had taken an orphanage brat into her heart and home was not there to offer the needed moral support. She had remarried a year earlier and moved to a trailer park in Arizona, beginning a new life with a retired FBI agent ten years her junior. Dear Aunt Helen had always welcomed a challenge. The labels that had once been put on Gabby—"hostile," "abandoned," and "difficult to place"—had only increased Helen Andrews's determination to succeed where others had failed.

Unfortunately, facing a chapel full of DeSpain relatives was simply too much of a challenge for Gabby. Coward that she was, it had been easier to run. Something inherited from her mother, perhaps—that nasty habit of leaving without a proper good-bye.

* * *

Pondering the possibility of her own insanity, Gabby sat on the beach until her legs were numb and the sun only a faint bloody tinge on the horizon. Her stomach rumbled with hunger, and had there been any food in her refrigerator, she might have summoned the energy to walk back to the rickety wooden steps that led to her humble abode. As it was, the refrigerator offered nothing more tempting than a tray of ice cubes. Her cupboards had also been cleaned out, as well as the warped armoire that passed for a closet. The word *home* possessed about as much appeal as an empty tomb.

Gabby heard a familiar asthmatic rattling behind her and felt a measured pricking and poking between her shoulder blades. Kitty wandered beneath her arm and sniffed her lap, settling finally in the wrinkled satin folds.

"Wha's'amatter?" Gabby idly stroked the crackling, plush fur. "Did you miss me, Kitty, hmm?"

"Actually," a husky male voice drawled behind her, "Kitty's rock went underwater. He was standing on his toes on the last dry pebble when I grabbed him."

Gabby whirled, dumping the cat headfirst into the sand. She gazed upward at what seemed to be an inordinate length of beautifully proportioned masculinity. Well-worn jeans molded lean hips and legs, soaking wet from the knees down. A wrinkled denim shirt hung outside his pants, buttoned haphazardly, the damp material stretching across an impressive width of shoulder and chest. Golden-brown eyes glittered oddly in the gathering dusk, taking their color from the dark blond hair splayed across his forehead. Darker brown sideburns blended with the stubble on his jaw, accenting the jutting chin and firmly molded lips.

Gorgeous but sloppy, Gabby scoffed silently, then colored furiously as she realized what a charming picture she herself made. Her hair twisted in wet, shiny snakes over her shoulders and smelled strongly of seaweed. A hysterical giant Siamese was climbing her back, intent on reaching the dubious safety of her head. And of course, she was wearing an elaborate wedding gown of mud and lace, a fact that had not escaped Tall, Blond, and Sloppy's notice, if his arrested expression was anything to go by.

Fighting satin skirts and a clinging cat, Gabby struggled to her feet, suppressing a very uncharacteristic impulse to burst into tears. Had she been a sane and rational woman, she would be on her way to Hawaii right now, basking in Alan DeSpain's calm serenity. That thought alone brought a gargantuan lump to her throat.

"Thank you," she muttered stiffly, dredging up the last pitiful shreds of her dignity. "I shouldn't have left him on that rock, but I thought he had more sense than to get stranded there."

"Hmm." The man's narrowed eyes roamed the length of Gabby's dress in apparent fascination, lazy amusement glimmering in their depths. "Is that what happened to the groom?"

"I beg your pardon?" Gabby paused in the act of dislodging the cat from her knees.

"The groom," the stranger explained patiently. "Did his rock go underwater, too? I hope he wasn't with the cat. I never thought to search for survivors."

Gabby closed her eyes for a moment, exhaling her

breath in a long-suffering sigh. She should have known. This blond buffoon put the finishing touches on an absolutely miserable day. What more could possibly go wrong?

"Excuse me." Stooping, she picked up the cat in one hand and the train of her gown in the other. Each movement was carefully executed with deliberate hauteur. There came a point when all one had left was pride. True, she might look like a visitor from the Outer Limits, but she certainly wasn't going to fall all over herself with explanations.

She drew herself up to her full five feet four inches, a challenging gleam in her eyes and a cold cat nose pressed against her cheek. "Thank you for saving my cat. I think I'll be running along now. I have more important things to do than provide comic relief along the shores of California." *Like going home and sucking on ice cubes.*

Her first step went very well. Gabby wasn't quite sure what happened beyond that point. Somehow her bare foot became tangled in the lacy underskirt of her gown, throwing her completely off balance. For an instant, she wobbled storklike on one leg, trying desperately to free herself. Kitty went sideways at the same moment Gabby pitched forward, coming up hard against a solidly muscled chest and strong supporting arms.

A lesser woman might have trouble dealing with this embarrassment, she thought wildly, struggling for air against the wrinkled denim shirt. She turned her head sideways, listening to the measured throbbing of his heart while she filled her lungs with tangy salt air. Other sensations slowly penetrated the chaotic state of her mind: warm breath stirring her hair, the scratchy beard against her temple, the cutting edge of a belt buckle pressed into her abdomen, and the unmistakable odor of alcohol . . .

Now Gabby knew what else could go wrong. No wonder those golden eyes seemed to glow with an inner light. The man smelled like the inside of a whiskey bottle.

Making sure both feet were firmly planted in the sand, Gabby placed her hands against the man's chest and shoved, putting twelve inches of fresh air between them. "You should be wearing a sign," she gasped weakly. "'Danger . . . Contains Flammable Liquid.'"

A flash of white teeth in the gathering darkness revealed that he was thoroughly enjoying himself, though when he spoke, his voice was laced with wounded innocence. "Surely you aren't accusing me of being drunk. I'll have you know I carry my liquor very well."

Gabby snorted inelegantly. "I'll bet. By the case, no doubt."

He took a step forward, sliding his hands into the pockets of his jeans. He studied Gabby through watchful eyes, a strange look passing over his face. Almost immediately, he was smiling again, with a smile that contained something of an apology. "Had I known I would be meeting my neighbor tonight, there would have been no need for the whiskey," he said cryptically. "Tell me, do you do this sort of thing often?"

Startled, Gabby eyed him warily. "What sort of thing?"

"Oh, slip into a wedding dress and spend the evening on the beach trying to drown your cat. Not that I have any objections," he added generously, indicating the sodden ball of fur now trying to climb his pant leg. "I never did like cats. I always thought there should be a hunting season for them, myself. Down, Sheba."

"His name is not Sheba and I wasn't trying to drown him!" Normally rather lukewarm toward four-legged animals herself, Gabby found the stranger's attitude inciting an unexpected surge of devotion for the stray cat that had apparently come included with the lease of her beach house. Instantly forgotten were all memories of the claw-shredded drapes in her bedroom, the cat hairs growing from her carpet, the dead mice that appeared magically on her doorstep every morning. Obviously, this disgusting man had no appreciation for an intelligent and loyal pet.

"It wouldn't surprise me to hear you own a very large dog," she said cuttingly. "A black drooling monster that eats cats for breakfast and enjoys a few beers before bedtime. Anyone who would actually suggest hunting..." Her voice faded in midair as the impact of his earlier words hit her. He had implied that they were neighbors. Gabby knew full well that there were no other habitations along this stretch of beach other than her own shabby dwelling and a sprawling redwood and glass ranch house situated on the cliff directly above them. The home itself was surrounded by immaculate grounds and a towering wrought-iron fence, creating an aura of wealthy privilege that had often intrigued Gabby. In her imaginings, she had visualized the owner as a rather effeminate-looking individual, sporting a clipped mustache and a luxuriant toupee. The man before her could not have been more than thirty-five years of age, and bore far more resemblance to a Viking warrior than a member of the idle rich. And Viking warriors, Gabby thought grudgingly, eyeing the snug-fitting jeans slung low on her neighbor's narrow hips, did possess a certain primitive attraction.

"You aren't by any chance renting, are you?" she asked curiously, her defense of the feline population all but forgotten.

He seemed to find the sudden change of subject perfectly natural. "I'm afraid not," he said regretfully. "I own that glass-walled monstrosity above us, although I do spend most of my time in Los Angeles."

Gabby studied him silently, feeling a distinct twinge of apprehension. It occurred to her that she could very well be standing on a deserted beach with an intoxicated schizophrenic who had delusions of grandeur. In other words, a lunatic.

He watched the play of emotions cross her face, noting the nervous flicker of her wide blue eyes. "I'm quite presentable when I get cleaned up," he offered mildly. "You should see me in a three-piece suit. I've been told I can be almost intimidating." He held out a hand, dangling it pointedly under Gabby's nose. "Michael Hyatt. Michael William Stanfield Hyatt the Second when I'm in my three-piece suit, plain old Mike when I'm rescuing cats in distress."

After a second's hesitation, Gabby reluctantly accepted his hand, feeling warm fingers close around hers. "Gabby," she replied automatically, wondering if all schizophrenics possessed such appealing smiles.

"I beg your pardon?"

"My name," Gabby explained, trying unsuccessfully to free her hand. The man had a grip like a pair of pliers. "Gabrielle Cates . . . could I have my hand back, please? Two have always been rather useful."

"I'm so sorry," he apologized solemnly. "I can't think what came over me. How do you do, Gabrielle Cates?"

"Fine, thank you." Never better, Gabby thought wryly, bending to retrieve her cat for the second time. Every woman's wedding day should be so memorable. "Well . . . it's been nice meeting you, Michael Hyatt. I think I'll take my poor cat home and put him to bed."

Mike nodded politely, rocking back and forth on the balls of his feet. "I assume you're a good swimmer, then?"

Juggling twenty pounds of shivering cat, Gabby staggered sideways on the sand. "Yes, I'm a good swimmer. Why on earth . . . *damn* you, cat, hold still . . . why on earth do you ask?"

He shrugged broad shoulders, looking at the stretch of beach on either side of their small cove. "Because I'm not. I only had to battle eighteen inches of water to save your cat, a risk I felt pretty safe in taking even in my . . . happy condition. It's only fair to warn you, I won't be diving in after you if you get into difficulties swimming home."

"Swimming home . . ." Gabby's voice trailed off weakly as a cold chill fingered her spine. She followed the direction of Mike's gaze, her eyes narrowed against the fading light. Foaming gray water surrounded them on all sides, lapping hungrily at the last few feet of dry sand on the beach. How could she have been so stupid? While she had sat and wallowed in self-pity the tide had risen, cutting off any means of escape from their rapidly diminishing mound of rock and sand.

"Well," Mike announced cheerfully, "every man for himself. Good-bye, Gabrielle. It's been a pleasure meeting you."

"Wait!" Gabby clutched at his arm in desperation, feeling her grip on both the cat and her sanity slipping. "Where are you going?"

"Up," he said simply. "Don't worry about me. This cliff looks sheer, but actually it's a fairly easy climb. I do it all the time."

"Don't worry about *you?*" Gabby repeated in astonishment. "What about *me?*"

"Well, you seemed so set on swimming..." He paused, running a thoughtful hand over the stubble on his chin. "I wouldn't want to disappoint you."

"Oh, a comedian. Just what I need," Gabby snapped irritably, brushing past him to stand at the base of the cliff. "How am I going to climb, carrying this cat?"

"You aren't." A firm hand reached over her shoulder, plucking the cat from her arms and dropping it on an overhang that jutted from the cliff directly above their heads. Instantly, the animal bounded up the rocky face, a bushy tail disappearing over the ledge thirty feet above them.

"So much for feline loyalty," Mike murmured dryly behind her. "After you, my lady."

What might have been an effortless scramble during daylight hours took on frightening proportions in the misty gray night. Hampered by a ten-ton wedding dress and frozen bare feet, Gabby continually slipped on the mossy stones and had to rely heavily on Mike's steadying hands on her waist and derriere. A third of the way up the cliff, she heard a muffled curse and felt the train of her dress being ripped from her skirt.

"Damn thing keeps trying to suffocate me!" Mike shouted above the wind that whipped sideways along the jagged face of the precipice. "Keep to the left now. Just feel above you for the handholds."

Gabby followed his directions, finding the ascent somewhat easier without the dragging weight of her train. The tender soles of her feet took most of the abuse of the climb, becoming raw and bloody long before Mike pushed her over the grassy ledge at the top of the cliff. Gabby rolled onto her back and stared blindly at the star-filled sky, drawing hungry gulps of air into her starving lungs. Her sleepy Siamese hunched over a nearby boulder, moonlight glinting off the tips of his white twitching whiskers.

"You're in lousy shape, but you're plucky." Mike blocked out the stars, looming over Gabby like God on Judgment Day. The wind slipped beneath his shirt, rippling the pale blue fabric.

Gabby, who had been sweating before, now shivered with cold. "Go—go away. My f-feet are bleeding and my legs . . . Lord, my legs. I can't feel them. I'm dying. Take care of my cat."

"I told you, I hate cats." Effortlessly, Mike pulled Gabby to her feet, swinging her into his arms. She gravitated to the heat of his body, murmuring a completely insincere request that he put her down immediately.

"Believe me," he grunted heavily, "I will put you down as soon as I possibly can. You weigh a ton in that ridiculous getup. If my house were any farther away, I would never attempt this impressive show of chivalry."

Perversely, Gabby thought his brutal honesty bordered on insult, and silently vowed to tell him so as soon as she found the energy. In the meantime, she found an odd sort of comfort cradled in his arms, her fingers splayed over the fine coating of sand that clung to his shirt. She closed her eyes tiredly and imagined herself in Alan's arms, being carried—calmly—over the threshold of the luxurious condominium he had rented in Maui...

It seemed only seconds later that they reached the wrought-iron gates that had always seemed so forbidding to Gabby. Mike maneuvered one hand free of her voluminous skirt, punching in a code on the illuminated security alarm. The double doors swung open silently, allowing them access to a shadowy garden. Gabby caught the tantalizing aroma of orange and lime, mingled with the softer scents of damp earth and flowers. She inhaled deeply, her nose twitching as she also identified the unmistakable odor of wet cat.

"We're being followed," she warned, knowing her pet's passion for central heating and plush carpets.

"I know." After a brief struggle, Mike managed to open his front door, swearing softly as a streak of gray fur shot between his legs, disappearing into the recesses of the darkened house. "Oh, hell, my Oriental rug... don't wiggle or I'll drop you."

"I can walk now," Gabby insisted, kicking at the yards of satin that enveloped her.

"I'm sure you can"—he paused for air—"but let's not try it just yet. I've got white carpet throughout the house, and I'm not wild about putting bloody footprints all over it. Hold those injured pinkies still until I get you to the kitchen."

"I'll try not to drip," Gabby muttered sarcastically, subsiding in his arms.

Mike picked his way unerringly through the darkness, dodging black, squatty-looking shadows that Gabby assumed were couches and chairs. They passed through swinging louvered doors and Gabby found herself dumped unceremoniously on a cold Formica bar. An instant later, the entire room was flooded with painfully brilliant fluorescent lighting.

"Good grief!" Gabby squinted against the sunbursts exploding behind her eyelids. "Does that light disinfect the room, too?"

Mike was standing by the light switch, near the swinging doors. His shirt was open to the waist, plastered to his body with sea spray and sand. His face was darkly tanned, a startling contrast to the ruffled blond hair that curled over the collar of his shirt. His tawny-colored eyes were hooded against the light, focused with a burning intensity on Gabby.

It began as a rumbling, a curious sound very much like the one Gabby's cat made after a particularly satisfying meal. Then the noise erupted from deep inside Mike's chest, unmistakable—and uncontrollable—laughter. Laughter that gentled the harsh angles of his face, laughter that gleamed in his golden eyes as he threw his head back.

Perhaps had she been less conscious of being the object of his hilarity, Gabby might have found the warmth and spontaneity of his laugh contagious. As it was, she had an overpowering urge to climb into a cupboard each time his eyes found hers and he lost control again. Rage and humiliation warred within her, with humiliation finally winning the day. She caught sight of her reflection in the gleaming window of a built-in microwave oven, blinked once, and burst into tears.

"I'm sorry," Mike managed between gasps. "Believe me, I didn't mean to laugh. If you could only see yourself—"

"I *can* see myself," Gabby blubbered. "Right over there, in your damned oven door! I've got dirt on my face and mascara running down my cheeks, and my hair looks like the coiffure of Frankenstein's bride. Which seems appropriate, since I'm dressed for the part as well."

He was beside her now, making an admirable effort to control himself. "It's not that bad," he said soothingly, only the slightest tremor running through his voice. "It was just the combination of the wedding dress and those poor battered feet and the seaweed on your head—"

"Seaweed," Gabby echoed dully.

"Just this one"—he pulled something long and slimy from her hair—"bit. There we go, down the drain. Now dry your blue eyes. You have my sincere and humble apologies for laughing at you. I'm a turkey."

Gabby looked sadly at the blood-encrusted toes peeping from the hem of her dress. "Don't apologize. I deserve this, really. I deserve every bit of it. Poor Alan. How could I have done this to him?"

Mike rummaged in a cupboard beneath the drain, bringing forth a dusty first-aid kit. "Found it. Swing your legs up on the drain so I can get to your feet. Who's Alan?"

Gabby did as he instructed, biting her lip as he brushed the sand and grit from the soles of her feet. "Ouch . . . that hurts. Alan's my fiancé. At least, he was my fiancé until this morning."

"Put your feet in the sink. I can't take care of the cuts until we wash the sand off. So what happened this morning?"

By the time her feet were soaked, swabbed, and bandaged, Gabby had verbally run the gamut of the entire wretched day, prompted by an occasional, well-placed comment from her attending physician. Mike refrained from passing judgment at the end of her tale, offering only a mild, "Poor fellow," which Gabby assumed applied to Alan DeSpain.

As it had been nearly twelve hours since her scanty breakfast of juice and toast, Gabby had no objections when Mike produced a makeshift meal of chicken sandwiches and steaming hot coffee. Mike's idea of a sandwich was to slap a thick piece of chicken on an even thicker slice of bread, smothering the whole with a generous layer of mayonnaise, but it was filet mignon to Gabby's empty stomach.

Mike sat across from her at the glass and chrome kitchen table, watching in horrified fascination as she devoured the last of three chicken sandwiches. "Tell me," he said finally, "does a guilty conscience always give you such a healthy appetite?"

Gabby frowned at him, fighting a sudden sleepy languor. "Guilty conscience? Oh . . . you mean Alan."

"Mm-hm." Mike smiled gently. "Remember him? Terribly understanding, wonderful in emergencies, salt of the earth?"

"Well, it's probably the best thing that ever happened to him. Any woman who would do this sort of thing twice certainly isn't good enough for Alan."

Mike's cup stopped dead halfway to his mouth. "Twice? You've jilted the poor guy *twice?*"

"Well, of course not." She dismissed the idea with a wave of her hand. "How could you even suggest such a thing? Alan is one of the finest—"

"I know all about Alan," Mike interrupted in a tone that indicated he was heartily sick of the subject. "And I didn't suggest it, you did. You said you had thrown him over twice."

"I did no such thing. I was referring to Zack." Gabby idly picked at the crumbs on her plate.

"Zack," Mike repeated faintly. "You mean, before Alan—"

Gabby nodded sadly. "Zack. He was a tennis player. I took one look at his blue eyes and I never knew what hit me. It was one of those whirlwind romances I'd always heard about and never really believed in. After only three weeks he asked me to marry him, but I just wasn't sure . . ." Why was she telling him these things? She was running off at the mouth like a waterfall. "Mike?"

"Yes?" His eyes were riveted on her, champagne-colored in the harsh white lighting.

"Did you put something in the coffee? I don't normally

. . . I feel kind of strange."

"A shot of whiskey, just to warm you up. You were saying?"

She stared at him blankly, fingering the tiny pearl buttons that closed her dress from neck to waist. "I don't remember. Oh, yes. Zack. We decided to move in together. I got as far as the front door. Where are you going?"

"Aspirin." He stood, pushing his chair gently beneath the table. "I feel a headache coming on."

"Hangover," Gabby murmured wisely. "You're going to pay for your sins, Michael Hyatt."

Aspirin bottle in hand, he slanted her a look over his shoulder. "In spades," he said with a glimmer of amusement. "In spades, Gabrielle Cates."

Chapter

2

GABBY DRANK TWO more cups of coffee before she realized her toes were numb.

"Oh, please, no more," she said when Mike hovered over her with the coffeepot. "I can't even wiggle them."

Mike dropped easily into his chair, his hands clasped behind his neck as he studied Gabby thoughtfully. "The mind boggles," he said. "What can't you wiggle?"

"My *toes*. They're always the first to go. Mike, just how much whiskey did you put in the—"

"I told you. Only a drop or two, certainly not enough to render you toeless. Besides..." Now he leaned forward, elbows propped on the table, one palm cupping the stubble on his chin. "I'm more interested in your cold feet than your numb toes. Tell me, was Zack as understanding as Prince Alan?"

Gabby accidentally conjured up a vision of Zack, blue eyes blazing, hands gripping her shoulders, horrible angry words turning to steam in the bitter December air.

"No," she said softly, talking more to herself than to the quizzical stranger opposite her. "No, he didn't understand."

"Ah, well. I suppose everyone can't be endowed with all of Alan's sterling qualities. I have to sympathize with your tennis player, Gabrielle. You do seem to have a little difficulty taking the—ah, plunge."

That was what Zack had said, Gabby reflected glumly. *You're a fake, you know that, babe? You hold both hands out and back up at the same time. If anything good ever happened to you, you wouldn't be around long enough to know it.* He had thrown her suitcases down the front steps of his apartment building, and the neighborhood children had cheered.

Mike's burnt-honey eyes studied her face with lazy amusement. "What is it with you? Normally it's the other way around, the man running for cover while the woman snaps at his heels."

"Then I'm the exception." Gabby dropped her eyes, staring at the blue-white diamond on her left hand. *The exception.* What an interesting—and painfully apt—description. "I forgot to return Alan's ring," she said tonelessly. "I'll have to take it to him."

At that moment, Mike nearly jumped off his chair, slamming his knees into the glass tabletop. "What the— something bit my ankle."

"Kitty." Gabby yawned again, unperturbed. "I saw him wander under your chair a minute ago. Something about men's socks rubs him the wrong way. He used to bite Alan all the time."

"Well, something about that cat rubs me the wrong way. I think it's the fact he's breathing." Mike ducked his head and glared at the contented animal who was settling himself over Gabby's bandaged feet. "What's his name? If I'm going to hate him, I need to know his name."

"Kitty."

"That's no name. Cats are named Snowball and Felix and Topaz."

"Well, mine is named Kitty," Gabby snapped, feeling herself at the end of an emotionally frayed rope. "It seemed logical, you see, since he's a cat. What marvelously inventive name did you come up with for your dog?"

"My dog?" For a moment, Mike looked dumbfounded, then a slow smile creased the shadow on his cheeks. He had a dent in his chin, Gabby noticed, where the dark brown beard did not grow. "Oh, yes, the dog." He nodded. "The black monster with a saliva problem. You were wrong there, Gabrielle Cates. I don't have a dog, beer-guzzling or otherwise. I live in a high-rise in Los Angeles that has strict rules about four-legged pets and two-legged children, rules that I support wholeheartedly."

"So you dislike pets and children," Gabby mused, curling her toes into Kitty's fur. "W. C. Fields would have loved you. Just out of curiosity, how do you feel about the hallowed institution of marriage?"

He flashed her a beatific, self-satisfied smile. "The very thought makes me break out in a cold sweat. As a matter of fact, my overindulgence with the whiskey bottle this evening was a direct result of a marriage-minded woman."

Despite her depression, the stinging needles of pain in her feet, and the beginnings of a throbbing headache, Gabby found herself chuckling softly. "Some poor girl wanted to tie the knot and you objected?"

"Violently."

"So you ran away to your beach house and hid behind its electronic gates."

"I have never been so grateful for this particular piece of property," he admitted. "More coffee? I'll make a fresh pot, free of intoxicating impurities."

"No, thank you. I'm waterlogged already." Gabby pushed her chair back and stood up with a groan. Her kneecaps had disappeared and the muscles in the back of her legs pulled in growing, numbing agony. "Gad, twenty-seven can't be *that* old . . . Mike, can I beg a ride home from you? If I don't soak my poor body in a hot bath, I'm going to be paralyzed forever."

Mike carried dishes from the table to the sink, whistling softly. "You ought to exercise more. Our little climb just wasn't that tough. You're out of condition."

"I'm a copywriter," Gabby said defensively, taking a few hesitant steps. Thick gauze cushioned her feet, allowing her to walk with a minimum of discomfort. "At least, I was a copywriter, until I quit because I was about to marry Alan. I sat at a desk all day writing paeans of praise to mouthwash and oven cleaner. I didn't get much exercise doing that kind of thing, so it's not surprising I'm in bad shape. Besides which, I'm basically lazy."

Mike leaned indolently against the counter, watching her tentative progress across the tiled floor. "I didn't say you were in bad shape," he corrected softly. "I said you were in bad condition. There is a world of difference there, Gabby."

"About that ride home," Gabby reminded him, dismissing a faint prickle of alarm. No man in his right mind would make a pass at a woman with two bandaged feet and a creeping case of paralysis.

"Sure." He patted the front and back pockets of his jeans, a frown creasing his forehead. "Must have left my keys upstairs. Hang on while I get them."

"Mike?"

He turned, dropping his hand from the swinging door.

"I never did thank you," Gabby said, her voice husky with fatigue. She met his light-filled eyes and tried to smile, then found she hadn't the energy.

A strange sort of stillness settled between them. Gabby heard the cat purring beneath the table, wheezing and rumbling in perfect time with the muted ticking of the kitchen clock. The overhead light tangled in Mike's hair, turning it the soft colorless beige that belonged to children's curls. It gave an odd vulnerability to the man who looked at her with heavy-lidded knowing eyes above a day's growth of beard.

Gabby shivered, suddenly cold. She felt exposed, trapped on the icy kitchen tiles, surrounded by walls of reflective glass and stainless steel. Only Mike's eyes were alive and warm, drawing her own like a flickering fire on a cold, moonless night.

His crooked smile snapped the tension and Gabby remembered how to breathe again. "You're in no condition to thank me tonight," he informed her wickedly. "But hold that thought. I'll be around a few more days. Hey . . . are you all right?"

Gabby opened her eyes, completely surprised to discover she had closed them in the first place. "My word, I seem to have fallen asleep standing up. I thought only horses did that."

"Come along, Sleeping Beauty." Mike's arm was around her, leading her from the kitchen, down the gray tunnel hallway and into the shadows of the living room. "I have a nice soft couch in here, just your size. It may save you from a concussion, falling asleep on your feet. There we go." He pushed her gently backward, watching as she settled into the feather-soft cushions.

"I'll never get up again," Gabby moaned, leaning her head against the enormous pillows scattered over the back of the sofa. "Every muscle in my body is screaming at me. You should have left me on the beach to drown, Michael Hyatt the Second. It would have been kinder. Is your couch made of marshmallows?"

Mike leaned over her, resting one hand on the arm of the sofa. His eyes wandered over her face for a long moment, noting the bruised shadows beneath her eyes. "You're beat," he said gently. "There are circles under your eyes big enough to swallow them."

By now he was so close she could feel the warmth of his breath on her forehead. She closed her eyes and savored the sensation, not at all surprised when she felt the light brush of his lips against the corner of her mouth. It was comfort and companionship, and she suddenly craved it.

She turned her head fractionally, moving her mouth over his in a soft, dreamlike eddy. He responded with an almost imperceptible pressure, rocking his head from side to side with an exquisite languor. There was no urgency to their movements, none of the hungry desperation that might have jolted Gabby from her sweet velvet darkness.

When Mike raised his head, Gabby's eyes remained closed, lips parted, one fist curled drowsily against her cheek. She was conscious of a vague feeling of loss, then decided dreamily that she must have imagined the whole experience. She drew herself into a fetal position on the sofa, burrowing into the tumbled pillows. She had no intention of sleeping. For now she would simply rest while Alan found his car keys. No . . . not Alan. She tried to gather her scattered thoughts. Stupid, to lie here while Alan waited at the church . . .

Gabby frowned, and drifted off to sleep.

The crack of thunder pulled her from her dreams. Gabby raised her head, totally disoriented for a dazed moment. An afghan was tangled with her legs, and the bulky skirt of her wedding gown was bunched beneath her hips. Her eyes felt gritty, as if they were filled with sand. She licked her lips with a flannel tongue and tasted salt.

The circumstances of her almost-wedding night returned to her in disjointed flashbacks, prompted by a faint throbbing in the soles of her bandaged feet. She groaned soundlessly as she recognized the muted glow building behind the living-room drapes. Daylight. She had slept the night through on Michael Hyatt's sofa.

She had a brief wrestling match with the afghan and discovered her muscles had atrophied during the night. The simple. act of standing on her own two feet took three practice runs and an assist from a floor lamp. Apparently, her body was holding a grudge for the unaccustomed exercise of the night before.

Bowlegged for the first time in her life, she padded to the window, parting the heavy curtains. Milky clouds leaked over a gunmetal ocean. Again she heard thunder, almost indistinguishable from the angry sounds of a white-capped surf. The cloud cover seemed too high and pale to indicate a major storm; more likely a heavy mist would linger along the beach until the afternoon sun burned it away.

Storm or no storm, she had definitely outstayed her welcome. Gabby knew from her frequent ramblings along the beach that Mike's house possessed a twisting set of stairs that, like her own, were useless during high tide. Now, however, the tide was out and the pathway clear along the beach. With any luck, she could leave without disturbing Mike, whom she assumed was sleeping in one of the upstairs rooms.

There was no sign of Kitty. Gabby considered quietly searching the house and then thought better of it. She could return later to collect her pet, as well as thank Mike properly. For now, it seemed far more important that she do a quick disappearing act before her reluctant host arose and felt obliged to offer her breakfast. Eating pancakes and eggs in a wedding gown would be simply too much to face.

A pair of men's slippers tucked partially under a recliner caught her eye. She hesitated, then slipped her feet into the warm sheepskin. Michael Hyatt might not thank her for borrowing his slippers, but her poor battered feet would be eternally grateful.

She fumbled with the latch on the front door, impatient to be gone. She wanted coffee, a hot shower, her toothbrush. She hardly noticed the rain beading on her eyelashes and drizzling down her neck. The iron gate surrounding the grounds gave her a moment's pause until she realized it could be opened from the inside without any need for the security code. The breeze pushed gently into her back as she negotiated the redwood stairs in flapping slippers. The clouds in the west were building up. A brisk squall of wind and rain was just what she needed to polish off this whole adventure.

Thunder rolled in from the fog and Gabby began to run, leaving dragging, clumsy footprints in the water-packed sand.

The telephone was ringing when Gabby unlocked her front door. It was Alicia, sacrificing her morning coffee break at the ad agency in the interest of burning curiosity.

"I've got nine minutes," she warned in a stage whisper, "so talk, and talk fast. What on earth got into you yesterday? One minute I was helping you with your veil, the next minute you were gone and Alan's mother was having a dizzy spell."

"I changed my mind," Gabby said in a hollow voice. "It was ... a mistake from the beginning. I should have known."

"Should have known? Should have known what? You and Alan were perfect for each other, you said so yourself! What *happened?* Why the disappearing act?"

Gabby was suddenly cold, her skin prickling. "Alicia, I can't explain," she said huskily. Then, before Alicia could fire another barrage of questions: "I take it Alan's mother was upset?"

There was a brief silence, then Alicia spoke again, her tone somewhat lighter and the demanding edge gone from her voice. "Oh, just a wee bit. She collapsed on the front pew and hyperventilated. I'd always heard that when someone does that you're supposed to put a paper sack over their head, but she fought me like the devil when I tried to put one on her."

"I completely forgot about her. I should have explained, but all I could think about after I'd talked to Alan was getting out of there. I suppose I should visit her and try to apologize."

"You'll have a tough time trying to find her at home," Alicia warned dryly. "Alan calmed her right down when he suggested she accompany him to Maui for a nice rest."

"Alan had prepaid for a week at the condominium," Gabby explained automatically, trying to assimilate the fact that Alan's mother had taken her place in Hawaii. "I suppose he didn't want to waste the money. Alan's always been very careful with a dollar."

"Alan has so many dollars to be careful with! Where were your brains, girl? Wouldn't it have been kinder to the poor man to marry him and then divorce him, rather than leaving him standing at the altar?"

"California's community property laws wouldn't have anything to do with your attitude, would they?" Gabby and Alicia had worked in the same department at Freed Advertising for nearly a year, and Gabby had become well acquainted with the avaricious side of her friend's nature, as well as the impulsively generous side. Alicia lived to marry money, regardless of the package it came in. She would find it very hard to come up with a good reason not to marry someone like Alan DeSpain. Not only was he extremely wealthy, but the package was so nicely wrapped.

"Certainly they do," Alicia responded firmly. "My word, you would never have had to work another day in your life. I can't see how marrying Alan would have been such a tremendous price to pay. He's rich, handsome, considerate . . . I could put up with that, I truly believe I could."

"Your chance will come. In fact, Alan's probably open to suggestions, if you have a mind to console him."

"Amazing. Yesterday you were going to love, honor, and cherish him forever, today you hand him to me on a silver platter. You've made a remarkable recovery, m'dear."

Gabby stared blankly at the calendar pinned to the kitchen wall. Yesterday's date had been circled with a red heart. "Maybe I'm just immune to the disease."

"Why, oh, why, did the Lord waste such a beautiful face and body on someone as selfless as you?" Alicia moaned. "If I hadn't already taken my vacation time this

year, I swear I would hop the first plane to Maui and let
Alan cry all over my body. As it is"—Her voice dropped
to a low growl—"I am chained to my desk. Without you
here at the agency, I'm completely swamped with work.
You should see the ding-a-ling Harrison hired to take
your place. She doesn't know beans about copywriting,
but she has terrific qualifications from the neck down."

"I know the type," Gabby said dully. Alicia's words
had come as a shock, though there was certainly no
reason that the agency should have hesitated to fill her
position on the off-chance that she would decide not to
get married. They had no idea that she was dangerously
unbalanced. "To the casual observer," Gabby mumbled
aloud, "I probably appear perfectly normal."

"What? I can't hear you. Dolly Parton has the copy-
machine going."

"Nothing. I was just thinking how nice it was going
to be lazing around until I find another job." After splurg-
ing on her trousseau, she had approximately five hundred
dollars in the bank. That gave her about four weeks of
lazing before she starved to death.

"Oh," Alicia said. "Yeah, that would be nice. This
nine-to-five bit can really get you down. Listen, I've got
to run. Harrison is giving me the evil eye. Come to lunch
Saturday. I'll fill you in on all the office gossip."

"Sounds great." Gabby's attempt at bright enthusiasm
fell flat.

There was a brief silence at the other end of the line,
then Alicia ventured carefully, "Gabby? I just want you
to know I'm sorry. I've played down this thing with Alan
because I thought it would be easier for you. I don't

know why it didn't work out between you two, but...
well, I'm here if you ever need to talk. I hope you know
that."

"Thanks, Alicia. I'm fine, honestly. And I'll look
forward to Saturday."

Alicia said good-bye, and the line went dead. For a
moment, Gabby stared at the receiver cradled in her
hands, wishing she had told Alicia the truth. But then,
what was the truth? Other than an industrial-sized depression fueled by guilt and regret, the abrupt death of her
relationship with Alan had been remarkably easy to bear.

No more painful, she recalled numbly, than walking
away from Zack had been two years earlier. Face it,
Gabrielle. You loved Zack's laugh, his athlete's body,
the crazy romanticism that inspired him to send roses in
December and give Easter baskets on Valentine's day,
but you were never in love with him. Alan cherished you
like some rare piece of porcelain and would have kept
you warm and safe forever, yet you never really needed
him. You tried, you tried so hard you almost convinced
yourself, but it just wasn't there. In the end, you simply
walked away, without a backward glance. In the end,
you'll always walk away.

Damn you, Momma. Look what you've done to me.

After showering, replacing the bulky gauze bandages
on her feet with thin plastic strips, and guzzling three
cups of instant coffee, Gabby felt half-human again. She
dressed in faded jeans and a USC sweatshirt, both relics
of college days gone by and the only articles of clothing
still hanging in her closet. She had every intention of

returning to Mike's house for Kitty, but no act of God or nature could convince her to do it before she found her makeup kit in the piles of luggage scattered throughout the house. Her ego had taken enough abuse, thank you.

She was head first in a box struggling to untangle the cords of her curling iron and blow dryer when a sharp knocking rattled the front door. Gabby groaned and straightened, brushing off her dusty knees. With Alan in Hawaii and most of her acquaintances under the impression she was with him, she knew of only one visitor likely to arrive at eleven o'clock in the morning. Kitty must have done something unspeakable to Michael Hyatt's Oriental rug.

She took a quick look through the peephole, recognized the unblinking Siamese held in the strong brown arms, and swung the door wide.

Mike smiled grimly over Kitty's silver-gray fur. He was clean-shaven and combed, a tiny nick still bleeding in the center of his chin. He wore biscuit-colored jeans and a white sweater, the sleeves casually pushed up above the elbow. A Saint Christopher medal glinted around his neck, matching the deep burnished gold of the watch around his wrist. He fairly dripped with understated elegance and bore absolutely no resemblance to Gabby's bearded and damply wrinkled climbing partner of the evening before. *Beauty and the Beast.* Gabby's ego whimpered under this fresh assault.

"You seem to have forgotten something, Gabrielle Cates."

His drawling voice was matter-of-fact, the lion-colored eyes filled with rain-washed light. Moisture had settled on his hair like a misty net, varnishing the thick golden strands. Beyond the covered porch, the rain and fog swirled in a boiling gray curtain, reducing the world to five square feet of peeling, white-painted plywood.

"I don't suppose you would believe me," Gabby ventured hesitantly, "if I said I was just coming to pick him up?"

"Of *course* you were." One long index finger idly flicked the cat's gray-frosted ears. "And you were going to bring my slippers back, too."

The slippers. She still wore them, and deep-pile sheepskin had never felt more uncomfortable. "Certainly I was. I would have asked if I could borrow them, but I didn't want to wake you."

He tilted his head, regarding her with a mixture of indulgence and impatience. Astonishingly, the hand that had been caressing Kitty now reached toward Gabby, tracing an invisible line along the dusky hollow beneath her cheekbone. "I was going to speak to you about your furtive little escape this morning. Didn't anyone ever teach you the proper etiquette for The Morning After? It's extremely rude to run off before breakfast, and the gentleman always escorts the lady home. It's probably a good thing you didn't marry Albert. You need more experience."

"His name is Alan," Gabby said faintly, feeling the touch of his hand long after he had gone back to tickling the cat. "And if you think you're going to goad me into telling you all about my vast experience with men, you have another think coming. Have you been drinking again?"

"I never drink before lunch." He glanced over his

shoulder at the drizzling sky, hoisting the cat under one arm. "It will probably clear up before long, but on the off-chance that it doesn't, can I come in?"

"Oh . . . of course." Gabby shuffled backward, allowing him to brush past her into the cluttered living room. Her nostrils were briefly tantalized by the elusive scent of musk cologne. Oddly enough, it made her far more uncomfortable than if he had turned up smelling like a distillery. "Watch out for the boxes. I'm in a bit of a mess here."

"I noticed. Where would you like the cat?" His face brightened with sudden inspiration. "Have you a garbage disposal?"

Gabby shut the door, throwing him an exasperated look over her shoulder. "I can't believe you hate cats as much as you pretend. No, don't put him on the couch, he shreds it. I'm teaching him to stay off the furniture. Just put him on the floor."

Mike did as he was told, watching with grim satisfaction as the cat immediately jumped up on the worn velvet sofa. "Ah, yes. A well-trained pet. Have you ever read the book, *One Hundred and One Uses for a Dead Cat?* It's a literary masterpiece."

"You're disgusting." Despite herself, Gabby began to laugh, the low, melodious sound lost in a sudden gust of wind that rattled the tiny frame house. Gradually, the elements subsided, leaving a suddenly strained silence and a smile that seemed stuck on Gabby's face. Across a sea of boxes and clutter, Mike watched her with disturbing concentration.

"You're staring," she said crossly. "It's rude to stare."

"That all depends on what you're staring at." Mike grinned, two deep grooves slashing either side of his hard brown cheeks. Weak sunlight filtered through the bay window to his left, gilding his hair and the soft white of his sweater. "I see only beauty," he intoned piously.

You should be looking through my eyes, Gabby thought, gazing at the man who wanted to put her cat in a disposal. If men could be called beautiful . . . or stunning, breathtaking, even downright bone-chilling . . . this man could qualify.

She cleared her throat and kicked at a stray curler on the rug. "It's also rude to be sarcastic," she said dryly. "I can't find my makeup bag, and my clothes are still packed. Even if I unpacked them, I couldn't wear them until I find my iron. I have very good reasons for looking like this. You probably won't believe this, but I'm usually a very organized, in-control type of person."

"You're right," he said. "I don't believe it. Tell me something, are you a very bad housekeeper or are you moving?"

"Neither." Gabby hopped two boxes, circled Mike and his after shave, and swept a protesting Kitty off the couch. "Bad cat . . . I *thought* I was moving. When I left for the church yesterday, I was all ready to set up housekeeping in Orange County. This morning I'm just sort of wandering around, wondering what to unpack first."

Mike frowned at her, absently picking the cat hairs off his sweater. "Do you know what you need?"

"Some help?" she replied hopefully. "There are a few really heavy boxes—"

"I never exert myself on Thursday. What you *need*"—

the last word was drawn out to give it the proper emphasis—"is to forget your messy house in a mindless whirl of pleasure-seeking."

Gabby eyed him suspiciously. "It's barely noon. It's raining outside. Just what sort of mindless pleasure-seeking did you have in mind?"

His smile widened, catching her off guard right in the solar plexus. "Darned if I know. Put me in a dark room with candlelight and wine and I'm chock full of ideas. Rainy Thursdays are a bit more difficult, but there has to be something better to do than clean house. We'll improvise."

The man was a positive menace. He had the smile of a saint, the eyes of a devil, and the charm of a cocker spaniel. Gabby knew if she had any sense at all, she would hand him his slippers and say good-bye.

She tottered between impulse and rationality. "I'm very hungry," she whispered, suppressing a shiver as his fingertips brushed her collarbone. "I haven't eaten since last night, and there's no food in the house."

He sensed her weakening and pressed his advantage. "I will ply you with hamburgers and fries," he promised solemnly. "I will take you to the market and buy you carrots and steaks and orange juice and eggs. We'll go for a ride in the rain in my dearly beloved Porsche, and if you are very, very good, I may even let you drive it. How's that for creativity?"

"I haven't any other clothes to wear. You'll have to take me as I am."

"Oh, I will." He was only a movement away now, toe to toe with his own brown slippers and coming closer.

His voice had a curiously gentle inflection, soothing her senses like sweet wine. "I wouldn't have it any other way, Gabrielle. We're very much alike, you know."

"We are?" His hand strayed to her cheek, slipped beneath the silky ebony strands of her hair, and cupped the baby-soft warmth of her neck. Gabby stared blindly over his shoulder at the water-stained wall, feeling a sudden rise in the room temperature.

"We are." One strong finger lifted her chin, and Gabby saw her own reflection in Mike's clear golden eyes. "We're both charming, bright, fun-loving, and allergic to matrimony."

"You're prettier than I am."

"Adorable dimwit. Pay attention. It's very seldom two rebels find each other. I think we should make the most of it."

"And how do we do that?" Treading warily, Gabby lowered her eyes from the sensuous impact of his direct gaze, concentrating on the slightly irregular hump below the bridge of his nose. That nose had been broken once. The knowledge was vaguely comforting.

"We follow our instincts." His smile widened, sending Gabby's pulses thumping. "Lesson number one. Stop feeling guilty about Alvin. You would have been—"

"Alan. *Alan.*"

"Alan, Alvin, whatever. You would have been bored stiff within a month. It wouldn't have been fair to either of you. Alan will find himself a nice girl who will worship the ground he walks on and who will ask for nothing more from life than the opportunity to produce and care for a dozen tiny little Alans. She will revel in diapers, dishes, and the PTA. She will make him the happiest of men."

"And I wouldn't have?" It was absurd to feel injured, Gabby told herself, blinking at the moisture blurring her vision. Absurd, irrational, unhealthy . . . the very future Mike had just described had sent her running from her own wedding as fast as her feet could carry her. So she happened to be a woman who valued her freedom. Was that so terrible?

Mike closed his fingers over a handful of hair, applying pressure to tilt Gabby's head back. "What do you think?"

Gabby stared mutely down her nose at the small razor cut on his chin. Mike waited, retaining his stranglehold on her scalp. He appeared to be a very patient man.

"I *don't* think," Gabby said, and sniffed noisily. "If I could manage a few rational thoughts, I wouldn't be in this mess. Did I tell you I was out of a job?"

"No." The one word quivered with amusement.

"Don't laugh at me."

"I'm sorry." He apologized by brushing a butterfly kiss over her forehead. Gabby's toes curled in the sheepskin slippers.

"They hired someone to take my place already," she explained, quite loudly. "Which leaves me with a beautiful new trousseau, practically no money in the bank, and no income. And then there's you."

"Moi?" His eyes warmed, gleaming through weighted lids. His mouth shadowed hers, beautifully curved, tempting—oh, yes, tempting. *Gabrielle, have you lost your mind?*

"Have you heard the one about the frying pan and the fire?" Gabby's voice was husky, ragged around the edges. She tried to read the intent in his face, her brows drawn together in fierce concentration.

Mike accepted her scrutiny calmly. "What do you see, Gabby?"

Gabby considered the question for several moments before answering. "I see a little boy," she said slowly, "who probably used to tie firecrackers to puppies' tails and blame it on the little boy next door. Can I trust you, Michael Hyatt?"

"It was a cat," he whispered, "and I blamed it on the little girl next door." Before Gabby could react, Mike's mouth settled beautifully, perfectly over hers, halting her respiration, her thoughts, the mindless struggle that barely had time to be acknowledged before dying a sweet painless death.

Gabby had known; the lazy passion in his eyes and his voice had been undisguised, making him almost vulnerable in those few dragging seconds before his head bent to hers. In a brief flash of intuition, she calculated the odds, deciding it would be insane to experiment with this particular man even as his lips began to move over her own in a drugging, sensual rhythm.

Mike's warm hands followed the length of Gabby's spine, lingering in the sensitive hollow of her back just above her buttocks, pulling her against him. Gabby lost track of her own hands; they clung to his shoulders, kneaded the taut muscles of his neck, tangled in thick, sun-streaked hair. *Insane.* The pressure against her back grew, and their hips began to move in an age-old dance that left Gabby gasping for air. Mike groaned against her parted lips, his tongue outlining the warm, swollen curves, tracing the even line of her teeth, finally probing inward with soft, gentle strokes.

Gabby felt the heat curling and building in her belly, spreading upward in pulsing electric currents. His mouth tasted of salt air and spring rain, and the primitive scent of musk hung heavily in her senses. Insanity was marvelous, exquisite, addictive. Gabby wanted to be insane forever.

Mike's hungry kisses altered, growing tender, feather-soft on her cheeks, eyelids, the tip of her nose. Hands that trembled ever so slightly cradled her head, gentle thumbs sculpting the hollows beneath feverish blue eyes.

Mike took a deep breath, his eyes slowly drifting closed. His lashes were beautiful, Gabby thought, thick and spiky and dusted with twenty-four-carat gold. More beautiful than any man's eyelashes had a right to be.

"I think you can," he said thickly, his eyes still closed.

Gabby's thought processes were stymied, her nerve endings raw. "Can what?"

"Trust me." He looked at her now, seemingly in complete control, flashing the most amazing, impersonal, social smile. "I had to get that out of my system first, but now I can promise you with almost total certainty that I can be trusted."

"Insanity is contagious," Gabby breathed. "Almost total certainty?"

"For today," he amended. "Find some shoes, Gabrielle. I refuse to escort a woman who wears bedroom slippers."

Chapter

3

GABBY SPENT THE better part of the afternoon acquainting Mike with Kelly's Shop and Go, a small local market equipped with four shopping carts and a grandmotherly cashier who boasted more years than the antique cash register. If Gabby had ever questioned the authenticity of Michael Hyatt's privileged background, his bewildered attitude when faced with the simple task of purchasing food supplies dispelled any lingering doubts. Never had the expression "a bull in a china shop" been more apt. Mike wreaked havoc with the produce section, toppling pyramids of oranges and canteloupes when he insisted on removing fruit from the crucial bottom row. He demanded Perrier from the cashier, and was told in no uncertain terms that she spoke only English. Eventually, Gabby sent him to wait in his cherished black Targa and finished her shopping in record time, spurred on by the thought that he might grow bored and once again offer his assistance.

Afterward, Mike fulfilled his promise of nourishment, guiding his car with careful precision past the drive-in window of Big Top Burgers. They ordered cheeseburgers, french fries, and cherry turnovers from a talking plastic clown, eating in the car while the rain drizzled over the gray-tinted windshield.

Eyeing the small brown sack sharing her bucket seat that contained Mike's only purchase at Kelly's, a jar of roasted almonds, Gabby asked curiously, "Just what do you do for food in your big house on the ocean? I recall being fed a quite good chicken sandwich last night, but somehow I can't see you stuffing and basting."

"And you never will." Mike's back rested against the door, one booted foot propped carelessly on the plushly carpeted driveshaft hump. "I rank cooking right up there with cats and the flu. A woman comes in twice a month to clean the beach house for me. I telephoned her when I decided to come down this week. She had the kitchen stocked for an army and a chicken dinner in the oven when I arrived."

"The beach house?" Gabby shook her head, marveling at his choice of words. "I might call it a seaside cottage, or even a summer house—yes, I like the sound of that, a summer house. What do you do for a living when you're not visiting your summer house?"

"Make paper clips." He smiled, biting into a limp

french fry. "Has anyone ever told you that you have Irish eyes? Midnight blue, put in with dirty fingers."

Gabby glanced quickly in the rearview mirror, looking for smudges. Shining nose, naked face. "What do you mean, dirty fingers? I haven't even got mascara on."

He leaned toward her, cupping her chin in one gentle hand. Leather seats creaked, stretched, settled into silence. "You have no romance in your soul," he said solemnly. "Irish eyes are a beautiful clear blue, surrounded by sooty black lashes. A very rare combination. Do you want the rest of your hamburger, Irish?"

Mike charmed her. He kept Gabby smiling, off-balance, almost—but not completely—unaware of the sexual currents rippling between them through the damp and foggy afternoon. He revealed very little about himself beyond a strong sense of the ridiculous and a passion for greasy hamburgers, preferring to discuss the most mundane details of Gabby's life. She found herself answering his questions as if the fate of humanity depended on a clear and concise answer. Did she enjoy parades, classical music, Mexican food? Did she always drown her french fries in catsup and pull the pickle out of her hamburger? Did she have much experience driving a stick shift, and if not, would she mind forgoing the promised treat of driving the Porsche home?

The afternoon lingered, stretched, ran reluctantly into evening. The rain drizzled into a heavy mist. Smog-colored sunlight filtered through spent clouds, carrying the first reddish smears of a watery sunset. Mike played Rachmaninoff on the car stereo and drove a sedate thirty miles an hour along the winding, rain-wet coastal road.

Gabby watched the ocean change from saffron to rust and snuggled deeper into the soft leather seat, content to live out the remainder of her days in this glorious car. Odd that she should feel such tranquillity on this, the most discouraging day of her life. She should be chewing her nails, agonizing over her future, *languishing*.

Instead, she fell asleep.

"You're destroying the mental image I have of myself," Mike said, unloading a week's supply of Tender Vittles from a bulging grocery bag. "My sparkling conversation and witty personality have put you to sleep twice now. Do you think you could manage to stay awake until I get to the bottom of this sack?"

"You should be flattered." Never one to stand when she could sit, Gabby sprawled in a rickety captain's chair, too well fed and relaxed to worry about the groceries cluttering her kitchen table. "You have that rare ability of putting people at ease. I never fell asleep with Alan."

Mike met her innocent look head-on, balancing a loaf of bread in one hand and a box of macaroni and cheese in the other. "Why, thank you," he said stiffly. "No doubt you meant that as a compliment."

"No doubt." The man had a face that stopped just this side of miraculous, a mansion for weekend jaunts, and a car that defied gravity. Apparently, he was also a stranger to humility. Gabby smiled to herself, liking him even better with his beautiful feathers ruffled. It was like seeing Robert Redford with a large pimple on his nose—somehow reassuring. It made one believe in the divine scheme of things. "You're squashing my Wonder Bread," she said sweetly. "Look, you really don't have to unload the groceries. It's very nice of you, but I can do it myself later."

"Ah, and here I thought you were beginning to understand me." Mike shook his head, delving into the bottom of the super-size, double-strength grocery bag. He came up for air waving a green-tinted wine bottle. "I never do anything without an ulterior motive."

Gabby's fingernails did a thoughtful tap-dance on the plastic tabletop. Mike smiled.

"I didn't buy that," she said. Then, after a brief pause, "Did I?"

"You didn't. I slipped it into your sack in the car. We're going to celebrate. Where are your glasses?"

"I have no idea." Gabby watched in fascination as he rummaged through the cardboard box on the floor containing her kitchen supplies. "What are we celebrating?"

"A variety of things. What's this?" He held up a very small glass pitcher with faded red markings.

"A measuring cup."

Mike grimaced, then shrugged. "There has to be a first time for everything. There's a certain romance to sharing wine from a measuring cup, wouldn't you say?"

"Oh, definitely." Gabby fluttered her eyelashes at him, a smile blossoming. "If only we had straws."

They sipped wine and ate roasted almonds and fought for leg space beneath the miniature kitchen table. They celebrated the Targa turning over ten thousand miles, drank a toast to Alan DeSpain's mother and a restful Hawaiian holiday, offered a tribute to unemployed copywriters the world over. Mike was raising the nearly empty cup to pay homage to Kelly's Shop and Go when the kitchen lights suddenly went out.

"An omen." His disembodied voice seemed to come from all corners of the cramped kitchen. "A store that fails to stock Perrier does not deserve a toast. Did you hit the switch, Irish?"

"No." Gabby's voice was strangely taut. "No. No, no, *no!*"

"Well, don't get hysterical. You probably just blew a fuse or something."

"Not a fuse," Gabby said faintly. "Oh, how could I have been so stupid? Why didn't I think? How could I have let this happen?"

"I must have missed something," Mike murmured. "I didn't think we'd gotten to that part yet."

"Don't you understand? I thought I was moving! I told them to shut it off!"

Mike popped another nut into his mouth, crunching thoughtfully. Gabby felt rather than saw his struggle to maintain a concerned and solemn attitude. "The electricity," he said finally. "You arranged to have the power company shut off your electricity."

"Such an organized bride," she confirmed miserably. "I did everything a bride-to-be was supposed to do except get married. Have you any idea what the power company is going to charge me to turn it back on again? What time is it?"

Mike consulted the illuminated face of his digital watch. "After seven. The power company is closed by now. You're in the dark until tomorrow morning."

"Damn!" Gabby slammed her palm down on the table.

Oranges rolled, hitting the floor with soft thuds.

"Feel better?" Mike asked kindly. "Abusing fruit is such a healthy way to deal with stress. Have you got a flashlight?"

Gabby blinked, her pupils gradually adjusting to the muted darkness. Mike had fluorescent hair, she discovered, each strand gleaming with the diffuse brightness of a tarnished halo. "No, I don't think so. There are some candles in the pantry. I didn't pack them, because they were already here when I moved in. I thought they might be the landlord's. Where are you going?"

"My car." Mike's shadow moved awkwardly around the table, hands groping before him. "I've got a flashlight and some matches out there."

Gabby winced as she heard the unmistakable sound of Mike's foot colliding with Kitty's litter box, followed by a thick silence. "Are you all right?" she ventured cautiously. "I forgot to warn you about the litter box . . . Mike?"

"Just counting my blessings," he rejoined tightly. "A broken toe is a small price to pay when you think I could have actually stepped in the—never mind. I'll be right back."

While he was gone, Gabby sat in the darkness and brooded on the possibility of existing without electricity until she found employment. Surely it wouldn't be so bad. A few meals of cold cereal and peanut-butter sandwiches, searching the want ads by candlelight, evenings spent by a cozy, crackling fire . . .

A vision of smooth brown skin, taut and glistening with a light tang of perspiration, crept up and startled her. Mike's skin, shimmering with the colors of a dying fire. Mike's hair, tangling and damply curling over light-filled eyes. Mike's hands...

What on earth was she doing? Gabby caught herself, pressing a trembling hand to the pulse jumping in her throat. Ruthlessly, she banished Mike's image from her mind, concentrating instead on dreary practicality. Her rental unit had no fireplace. And her curling iron, her indispensable Teflon-coated curling iron, ran on electricity. No way could she face the grueling task of job hunting without her curling iron. Perhaps the power company honored credit cards.

A milky beam of light heralded Mike's return, crawling across red and gray linoleum, climbing up Gabby's jeans, and lingering on the soft white flannel stretching lovingly across her breasts.

"Found it." Mike cleared his throat while Gabby shot to her feet. "The flashlight, that is. And the matches. The flashlight and the matches."

"You're a child, Mike," Gabby said crossly, trying to stem the quivery feelings in her chest.

"Innocent. Loving. Trusting." The light arched, illuminating his deceptively pure features. "How well you read my character. Where's your pantry, Irish?"

She led him to the oversize closet that boasted the grand name of *pantry,* holding the flashlight while he probed the recesses of the upper shelf.

"Incredible." Mike's voice echoed, faintly three-dimensional. "Will you look at that?"

Gabby stood on tiptoe, straining to see over his shoulder. "Look at what?"

"I've discovered the place where spiders go to die," he announced, à la Vincent Price. "Now I know how Howard Carter felt at King Tut's tomb. Want to take a look?"

"No." The single word was accompanied by a shudder.

Mike shrugged, passing her a dusty box of emergency candles. "Faint heart. It looks like there are only two candles left. We won't be playing any long poker games tonight. Unless..."

"Unless?" There was a breathless anticipation in Gabby's voice that she herself did not understand. The flashlight hung limply in her hand, revealing every scuff and stain on her aged running shoes in brilliant detail.

Even in murky shadows, the man's smile packed a wallop. Firm hands closed around Gabby's waist, dragging her gently toward a glinting belt buckle. Gabby's breath stopped, began to burn in her lungs. Mike pressed a baby-soft kiss on her nose, rubbing his forehead lightly against hers. "Are you a gambler, Irish?" he queried softly. "I know all sorts of games to play in the dark."

"Risky games?" Gabby asked. She could barely get the question through desert-dry lips. The flashlight and the candles crashed to the floor in ear-splitting unison.

"They can be." His hands moved beneath her bunched-up sweatshirt, spanning the soft, moist warmth above the waistband of her jeans. "But you know what they say. It's not whether you win or lose..." His fingers skimmed over her ribcage, feathering lacy patterns on hypersensitive skin. "It's how you play the game. How do you play the game, Irish?"

Gabby said something—a choked little exclamation that sounded like "help." Mike smiled. Lordy, that smile. This was a situation that called for quick thinking and a firm stand. But how could Gabby think when the sweet kindling pressure of Mike's hands was filling her head with desperate fantasies? Her breasts felt alien, swollen with a tantalizing heaviness. Her eyes hurt from staring in the darkness to see his face, and her pulse was a thready, irregular hum in her ears.

She temporized. "I've never been very good at games."

"How about follow the leader?" Mike sailed light kisses over the sculpted line of her jaw, down the velvet-soft curve of her neck. "A simple little game where everyone plays"—his mouth covered hers briefly—"and no one loses."

"I should pick up the candles."

"Or hide and seek." One of his palms slid upward, cupping and lifting the tender weight of her breast. His thumb made a shaky foray across her nipple, his long, sensitive fingers tightening convulsively until Gabby gasped with the pleasure-pain of it. "Irish..." He drew a shuddering breath. "You can find such nice surprises playing hide and seek."

"I may have broken your flashlight." All she could manage was a ragged whisper.

Mike shook his head mutely, effectively silencing any further reference to the wounded flashlight. His respiration seemed to have kicked into overdrive, and when he spoke, his voice was thick with raw edges. "I've been waiting," he said. "Have you been waiting?"

The million-dollar question, Gabby thought wildly, put with charming, deceptive simplicity. He talked of games and surprises and waiting like a polite child for a treat, and all the while his luminous golden eyes were tangled helplessly with hers and his hands were hungry on her body and desire spiraled feverishly between them.

Afterward, she could never remember her answer, never remember even giving an answer before Mike's mouth possessed hers with a deeper, more intimate contact. His hands tightened, pressing upward, and Gabby clung to him with a sudden, fierce greed. She was welcomed in the hard cradle of his arms, and it no longer mattered that they only played at love, because Mike's games were magic. His hair ran like watered silk through her fingers, cooling her heated palms. His hands molded her body, following her hips, stroking the curve of her spine, finding their way back again and again to the curve of her breasts. Gabby's veins ran riot with liquid fire and her limbs grew heavy with the aphrodisiac he fed her. Thought evaporated like steam. She went with him willingly, following his lead into the magical, sensual playground he seemed to know so well. And through the trance, Gabby heard bells. I'm dreaming all this, she thought.

His mouth left her own and Gabby sighed, bereft. He moved clumsy, passion-drugged hands to frame her face, and Gabby burned where he touched.

"Gabrielle . . ." He stopped, closed his eyes and began again. "Sweetheart . . . your bell is ringing."

"You heard it, too?" Gabby asked huskily. Could a dream be shared?

"Unfortunately. And whoever it is isn't going away. Persistent little beggar."

The doorbell. Gabby whirled, feeling like a total idiot.

There was something to be said for the old clichés after all. She had indeed been saved by the bell . . . and the knocking, and the angry shouting that threatened to drown out the ocean's rumble.

"I think I had better answer it." Mike frowned. "It sounds like you've got some looney on your front porch."

"Don't bother." Gabby sighed, squeezing her eyes tightly shut. How much could one woman take before she cracked? "I know who it is."

A muffled threat was voiced from the front porch, something about dogs and policemen and a rear end full of buckshot. "You actually *know* that person?" Mike asked slowly.

"I'm afraid so." Gabby picked up the flashlight, relieved to find that it still worked. Mike followed her to the front door, one hand resting lightly on her shoulder. Another threat greeted them as she struggled with the lock, the caller revealing a remarkably creative vocabulary.

"You have my sympathy," Mike said. "No one should know that fellow. Should I arm myself with a poker or something?"

Gabby choked and opened the door, biting her lip to kill a smile. The tall, heavy-set man on the stoop blinked in the sudden glare of the flashlight, raising a hand to shield his eyes.

"Mr. Paulsen," Gabby said tiredly. "Won't you come in? Mike, this is my landlord, Mr. Paulsen."

"Are you crazy?" Mike whispered. "He's a *giant*."

Fortunately, Mike's comment was lost in the barrage of accusations, questions, and demands that Mr. Paulsen issued during the next several minutes. At the best of times, Gabby's landlord was difficult. When he thought he was being taken advantage of—as he did now—he was impossible.

"I'm trying to explain," she interrupted for the third time. "I only paid the rent up until yesterday because I was getting married. I hadn't planned on still being here, I swear."

Mr. Paulsen snorted. "I'll bet. Until you realized what a cozy little place this would be for a honeymoon. And free of charge, at that. A romantic little hideaway, and no one the wiser."

"This man is insane," Mike said calmly. "Cozy? A romantic hideaway? Call the police, Irish."

In the hazy glow of the flashlight, Mr. Paulsen's color deepened to an unbecoming salmon. "Police? I'm the one to be calling the law! You thought if you kept the lights out, you could pull the wool over old Carl's eyes. Well, it didn't work, so pack your bags. You and Romeo here are lucky I don't turn you in for trespassing."

Gabby pressed her hand agitatedly to her forehead. "Please, if you would just listen for a moment—"

"And clean the place up!" Mr. Paulsen bellowed. "I've got a new tenant moving in on Monday. I want this place spotless, just the way it was when you moved in. And I want an extra day's rent. Now."

Gabby seldom cried. As a matter of fact, she had shed more tears in the last two days than she had in the last ten years. Apparently, it was getting to be a nasty habit. Mr. Paulsen's quivering jowls were fogged in a veil of tears. Wretched man. How to explain that she hadn't married, that Romeo wasn't her husband at all, that the electricity had been shut off . . .

No. Explanations were out of the question. It was clearly a case of the truth being more incredible than fantasy.

"Why don't you go make some coffee?" Mike suggested quietly. "Mr. Paulsen and I are going to have a little chat."

Gabby sniffed and studied the flashlight intently. "Can't. No electricity."

"Then make me a nice warm cup of tap water. No, you take the flashlight. I have excellent night vision. Now scram."

"Mike—" Gabby looked from Mr. Paulsen's massive build to Mike's leaner frame.

"Bye-bye, Irish."

Gabby sat quietly in the kitchen, listening. No raised voices, no sounds of furniture crashing against the wall. She heard the front door latch quietly, then waited while Mike shuffled his way through the darkness into the kitchen. Suddenly, Kitty yowled and Gabby nearly jumped off her chair.

"I stepped on his tail," Mike said innocently. "I'm terribly sorry. I can't see a thing in this light."

"I thought you said you had excellent night vision."

"Except for cats. You're off the hook, Irish. Paulsen has given you until Sunday to find somewhere else to live. Until then this romantic honeymoon hideaway is all ours."

"Mike, you didn't—"

He sighed. "No, I didn't. I spun him a heartbreaking

tale about how you were jilted by your fiancé on your wedding day. You know, I really have quite a flair for dramatics. I nearly had him in tears."

"If you think I believe that . . ." Gabby's voice thinned to a whisper as Mike's hands found her shoulders, gently kneading the taut muscles.

"You're right," he admitted. "I bought him off. You owe me twenty-eight dollars, Irish. Plus a forty-dollar security deposit."

Even under his skillful hands, her body remained tense. Her mind was whirling with the confusing fragments of her life, fragments that had fitted together so beautifully only two days before. How on earth had it all fallen apart? No marriage, no job, no home, no electricity. She was left with an overweight cat and a flaming headache— not to mention the debt of sixty-eight dollars she now owed Mike. Under the circumstances, there seemed to be only one appropriate course of action. She had to go to sleep before anything else happened.

"Mike . . ." Suddenly, it was an effort to even speak. She turned, mildly surprised that Mike's features revealed no trace of the passion she had seen earlier. A sympathetic smile glimmered in his tawny eyes, nothing more. Gabby began to wonder if she had imagined the whole experience. It wouldn't surprise her. Weren't hallucinations a prelude to nervous breakdowns?

"Find your candles," he said. "I'll light them before I go."

"You're leaving?" Gabby was relieved. Wasn't she? An orange rolled from the shadows, nudging her toe. Grateful to have an excuse for movement, she bent and picked it up, setting it carefully on the table. It wobbled, gathered speed, and dropped to the floor. Naturally.

"Candles," Mike repeated gently.

He placed them on Mason jar lids, setting one on the table and the other on the counter top. Gabby burned her fingers trying to help him light them, and he told her to sit down and stop being a pest.

"I'm off," he said. "Keep the flashlight and try not to burn down the house tonight."

Gabby watched him over a flickering yellow flame as he walked across the kitchen, this time making a wide circle around Kitty's litter box. She tried to think of the proper thing to say. Her brain balked, cold and sluggish, finally bringing forth that most original of all phrases, *We must do this again sometime*. She sucked on her injured finger and opted for silence.

Moonlight spilled weakly through the torn screen door. Mike turned in the chalky square of light, head tilted in a pantomime of thoughtful consideration. "If I asked you to stay at my place tonight, what would you say?"

"No."

"No?" he asked. "When I'm simply trying to be a good Samaritan?"

She looked away from his crooked smile, trying to reinforce the crumbling hold she had on her willpower. Her gaze dropped to the lean pure lines of his hips and thighs, muscles molded in soft, cream-colored denim. Mistake.

"Are you?" she queried huskily. *Discipline, Gabrielle.*

"A good Samaritan?" He pushed open the creaking screen door and flicked a quick wave in her direction.

"Hell, no. Goodnight, Irish. And try not to worry. Everything will work out."

Try not to worry. She sat in the kitchen long after he left, until the candles sputtered in their own tallow. Half-asleep, she finally decided it was very good advice. There were too many things to worry about to settle on any one individual problem.

Better to sleep. Which she did, on a bare mattress, wrapped in a bedspread and wearing Mike's slippers.

Chapter

4

"OH, PLEASE . . . THIS IS too much. I can't take it." Alicia was laughing too hard to move, doubled over her lemonade in a white plastic lawn chair. "What happened after he stepped in the litter box?"

"He *didn't* step in it." Gabby eyed her friend sourly over her own drink. "He stubbed his toe on it. Why do I get the feeling you aren't taking my sob story very seriously? Straighten up, Alicia, you're getting your hair in your drink."

"So I am." Alicia raised her head, her eyes swimming with tears. "Don't get huffy, a saint couldn't keep a straight face after a story like that. Where you find them all, I'll never know."

A Frisbee sliced the air between them, whistling past Gabby's ear. She took it all in stride, well acquainted with the Coppertone surf set that populated the enormous wooden apartment building where Alicia lived. Although the ocean was three blocks away, the spirit of the sand prevailed in the grassy court behind the apartments. Rock music underscored the hot and humid afternoon, surfboards shuffled back and forth with the tides, and the aroma of coconut tanning oil hung permanently in the air. Alicia had never learned to swim, and the smell of coconut oil made her queasy, but the modest rent she paid allowed her to indulge her passion for wickedly expensive lingerie and handmade Italian shoes. Alicia freely admitted to being something of a spendthrift; she looked forward to the day when a generous husband would provide the means to become a reckless spend-thrift.

"Don't know where I find who?" Gabby asked, pressing the frosty cold glass against her forehead.

"Men. No, let me rephrase that. *Interesting* men. Take it from the woman who went out with a balding podiatrist last night. Interesting men are hard to find, let alone rich, handsome, and single interesting men. Was he?"

Gabby sighed. "You're giving me a headache. Was he what?"

"Was he"—Alicia paused to appreciate a surfboard passing by with bronzed, muscular legs—"single?"

"Very," Gabby said. *"And* permanently, and what does that have to do with anything? Good grief, three days ago I got a speeding ticket running away from my own wedding. What did you expect me to do, stop off home to powder my nose and head out to the nearest singles bar?" Guiltily, Gabby reached for her napkin, wiping away her lipstick and the sensation of Mike's mouth wet-burned into hers. *She* understood perfectly well why she had been temporarily susceptible to Mike's particular brand of charm. She had been lonely and discouraged and he had offered her an emotional "pat on the back." It was as simple as that. Unfortunately, Alicia might misconstrue the situation.

"And that," Alicia pronounced dramatically, "is, as they say, the hell of it. I *did* spend last Wednesday night at a singles bar. That's where I met the podiatrist. You, on the other hand, retreated to a deserted beach and ran smack into the man of my dreams."

"He was drunk," Gabby said dryly. "He practically ripped my wedding dress to shreds and he threatened to put my cat in the disposal."

"Like I said"—Alicia grinned irrepressibly—"interesting. Did you ever get the electricity turned back on?"

Reality. Gabby squinted into a steel-blue sky and forced a tight smile. Electricity. Employment. Housing. Survival. The stimulating little challenges of life. "Not yet," she said evasively, unwilling to foist her very immediate concerns onto Alicia. She had deliberately omitted any mention of Mr. Paulsen's visit, likewise the anemic condition of her bank account. Old habits were hard to break, and the habit of depending solely on herself had long since become second nature. "I'll call on Monday. It's been kind of fun living by candlelight." *But it's a very inconvenient way of cooking macaroni and cheese,* she added silently.

Alicia shook her head, sunlight glinting on her rioting auburn curls. "You're amazing, the way you just sail through these things. I can't tell you how glad I am you came to lunch today. I've been worried about you, friend. I've had these awful visions of you sitting home alone, wringing your hands and crying over Alan's picture."

"Second thoughts?" Gabby smiled wistfully and shook her head. "It isn't in my nature. You know, I don't believe I have a picture of Alan."

Alicia's eyebrows rose. "Engagement photo?"

"Alan kept the prints. He wanted to save them in a Book of Remembrance."

"A Book of Remembrance," Alicia echoed with something akin to reverence. "And this is the man you let slip through your fingers. You don't mind if I shed a few tears, do you? I don't think I'm quite as adaptable as you are."

"Acquired talent," Gabby said lightly. Her velvet-black lashes dropped as she studied a bumblebee buzzing unsteadily over her lemonade. "And speaking of talent, tell me more about my so-charming replacement at the agency. Has she learned to type yet?"

Alicia immediately launched into a lively description of one Bunny Rosenthall, which led to a discussion of male mid-life crisis, which somehow turned into a debate on the best way to remove soap scum from bathroom tile. Gabby's cheeks and shoulders were stinging with sunburn when she finally headed her Volkswagen Rabbit homeward on Highway One. She drove slowly, partially because she was still drowsy from the summer heat and partially because she had no real desire to return to her empty cottage. She stopped at Kelly's Stop and Go to buy a newspaper and extra batteries for Mike's flashlight. Tonight was reserved for scanning the help-wanted ads and plotting her job-hunting strategy. Tomorrow she would find herself an inexpensive apartment, something within her very limited means. It was time to pick up the pieces and start over again. Somehow.

It was late evening, a moonlit, ocean-fresh evening, when Gabby finally returned home. At first she noticed nothing amiss. She walked slowly from her car to the back door of her cottage, listening to the soothing rhythmic sounds of the surf in the crystal-clear air. She would miss the ocean when she moved. She'd grown used to its comforting presence, the stark, majestic beauty of the rugged coastline, the stars that reeled across the sky in familiar glittering patterns. She could never remember actually having noticed the Big Dipper when she lived in Los Angeles. Perhaps she simply hadn't taken the time to look, or maybe the pollution had clouded the skies. She did know there was very little chance of finding another apartment near the beach on her limited budget. More likely she would end up in the sweltering inner city, with an excellent opportunity to observe firsthand whether or not the Big Dipper could be seen through a Stage Three smog alert.

Gabby was sifting through her purse for her house keys when she noticed the sliver of light glimmering through the crack in her kitchen curtains. Light? Had she forgotten and left the kitchen lights on? How on earth could she have done that when there was no electricity? Briefly, she considered the possibility that she had stumbled onto a burglary in progress, then dismissed the idea as absurd. No self-respecting burglar would be caught dead breaking into her pitiful little cottage. There was simply no incentive.

Just the same, her fingers trembled slightly as she gripped the doorknob. It turned in her hand, the door swinging open with a rusty staccato creaking. Surely she hadn't left it unlocked? Growing up in Los Angeles, one learned to lock doors with the same automatic reflex that governed breathing out after breathing in. Gabby swallowed through a painfully dry throat and wondered idiotically if the economy had affected the criminal element in California.

Her knees were knocking and she called herself a hundred different kinds of fool for even stepping through the doorway. The overhead lights were blazing in her little kitchen and a teapot was whistling on the stove. The burglar's purse was resting on the kitchen table.

The burglar's *purse?*

Gabby walked slowly toward the purse, feeling as if she had wandered into someone else's dream. The kettle began to rattle and shake on the stove, begging for attention.

"There you are," a feminine voice chirruped behind Gabby. "I was wondering when you'd get back. I'm Samantha."

Gabby whirled, gaping dumbly at the petite blonde standing in her kitchen, holding her cat and wearing her bathrobe. Her hair was damp and curling in fragile wisps around her forehead and ears. She was regarding Gabby with friendly sherry-brown eyes that crinkled at the corners when she smiled. She looked delicate and feminine and quite harmless.

"Hi," Gabby said faintly. "I'm Gabby."

"I know. The landlord told me all about you. You're here just in time, tea's ready." Samantha placed Kitty on the floor and shuffled across the kitchen in flapping, familiar slippers. "I hope you don't mind me wearing your robe," she said cheerfully as she pulled two cups from the mug tree on the drain. "I was just getting out of the shower when I heard the kettle whistling, and I grabbed the first thing I found. We're the same size."

Gabby dropped into a kitchen chair. "That's lucky."

"Except for our feet. Lord, you must wear a size fifteen. Wearing these slippers is like walking around in a couple of tugboats."

"They aren't mine," Gabby heard herself say. "They belong to a friend."

Samantha grinned over her shoulder. "I thought as much. Lemon and sugar?"

"I haven't any lemon," Gabby replied automatically. Her brow knit thoughtfully. "Come to think of it, I haven't any tea, either."

"Oh, I brought some. My favorite blend. Some people can't begin the day without a cup of coffee; I'm totally useless without my tea."

Five seconds of perfect blank. "You're staying the night, then?" Gabby asked finally.

Samantha giggled, setting two cups of tea on the table and returning to the counter for a plate of cookies. Familiar plate, unfamiliar cookies. "I'm sorry," she apologized, slipping into the chair opposite Gabby. "Here

I've been babbling on and I haven't even introduced myself properly. I'm Samantha Monroe, the new tenant. I know I wasn't supposed to move in until Monday, but I lost the lease on my other place and the landlord assured me you wouldn't mind if we shared the cottage for a couple of days. As a matter of fact, he practically insisted on it."

The pieces of the puzzle that was Samantha Monroe dropped quickly into place. "I should have known," Gabby said slowly. "Collecting a double rent would be irresistible, even if it was only for a couple of days. My beloved landlord makes J. R. Ewing look like Father Christmas."

"You think so?" Samantha pursed her lips and blew upward at a stray curl dangling over one eye. "I thought he was kind of sweet, myself."

Gabby choked on a mouthful of tea, the flavorful brew dribbling down her chin and onto her pink sweater. *"Sweet?"*

"Uh-huh. He couldn't have been more helpful. I called him when I arrived this afternoon and found there was no electricity. He took care of everything. The power was restored in less than thirty minutes."

"Good Lord," Gabby murmured. Life was just one surprise after another these days. "He must have hidden charms."

"Possibly." Samantha cocked her head to one side, brown eyes twinkling. "You know, you're taking all this remarkably well. Most people would have been a little irritated to find a complete stranger brewing tea in their kitchen."

"I'm adaptable," Gabby said. She told herself the

cookies were made with NutraSweet and reached for her second. "I have it on the best authority. Besides, when I realized you weren't a burglar, I was too relieved to be irritated. Better a stranger brewing tea in your kitchen than a stranger ransacking the drawers in your bedroom."

"Very true," Samantha said appreciatively. "I can't tell you how much I admire logical thinking. My family tells me I haven't a whit of common sense, myself. That's the reason I don't own a car. Street signs disorient me and I have absolutely no sense of direction. So I take buses and trains and leave the driving to all those logical types who have mastered the Santa Ana Freeway. I'm too emotional to make all those split-second decisions. I tend to react with my heart instead of my head, but I think in my profession that's an advantage."

Gabby was almost afraid to ask. "Just what is your profession?"

"I'm an actress. Thus far in my career, I'm known primarily for my teeth—I've done several toothpaste commercials—but my agent tells me the big break is just around the corner. Oh, and I died on *General Hospital* last week. I was one of the victims of a Rapid Transit disaster."

"That sounds encouraging," Gabby commented, hoping she had said the right thing. Apparently she had; Samantha glowed like a Christmas tree someone had just plugged in.

"It was terrific exposure. I was DOA, so I didn't have any lines, but I had a great close-up when they pulled the sheet over my face. I have the show on tape. I'll play it for you tomorrow."

Gabby's blue eyes had become very bright. "I'll look forward to it," she managed unsteadily.

Samantha was clearly delighted. She offered Gabby a fresh cup of tea and said impulsively, "He was right. You aren't at all what I expected."

Trying to keep up with her astonishing visitor's conversation was like trying to catch a runaway freight train. Impossible but invigorating. "Who was right?"

"Oh. The landlord." Samantha ducked beneath the table, reappearing with a Siamese stole slung over one shoulder. "He told me that you were one of a kind."

Remembering Mr. Paulsen's apoplectic fit, Gabby said wryly, "I don't think he meant that as a compliment."

Gabby smiled serenely and buried her nose in Kitty's fur. "Then again," she mused lightly, "maybe he did."

Today had turned into tomorrow and Gabby was yawning between every second word when she finally excused herself and went to bed. Samantha waved happily from her custom-squashed bean bag in front of the television, calling a cheery good night through a mouth full of popcorn. Gabby's temporary roommate had made herself right at home, brewing pot after pot of tea and chattering away with Gabby as if they were lifelong friends. What might have been an awkward situation turned into something resembling the Mad Hatter's tea party. Surprisingly, Samantha never asked the obvious questions that might have been difficult for Gabby to answer. Apparently, it never occurred to her to wonder why Gabby had been living without electricity, why cardboard boxes with Alan DeSpain's address were scattered throughout the house, or why a bedraggled wedding gown was hanging in the front hall closet. Samantha seemed to move in a sphere far above these mundane details, tripping through the house in Gabby's robe and Mike's slippers, enchanting Kitty with a belly rub, maintaining an artless, amusing flow of conversation that was remarkable for its triviality. It was impossible for Gabby to be depressed in her company, just as it was impossible to concentrate on the dreary chore of reading the help-wanted ads. Instead, like Scarlett O'Hara, she put off the problem of survival until tomorrow, applying herself instead to the really serious business of making popcorn balls and peanut-butter fudge, charting her horoscope, and watching reruns of *Masterpiece Theatre* and *M*A*S*H*. She accomplished absolutely nothing, an achievement that sent her to bed with a smile on her face. Mike would have been proud.

Gabby greeted the new morning with a junk-food hangover. Her fingers were sticky with caramel and blanket lint, popcorn was stuck between her teeth, and three pounds of fudge had settled permanently on her hips. She offered a silent prayer of repentance, punishing herself with a cold shower and a breakfast of ice water and vitamin pills. When Samantha finally emerged from the back bedroom, Gabby was hunched over the kitchen table, circling classified ads with a red magic marker.

"Morning." Samantha yawned, knuckling her eyes with her fists. She was wearing an oversize pink nightshirt that barely covered the tops of her thighs, the sleeves doubled over at the cuffs. Her face was flushed with sleep, and mascara was smudged beneath her eyes. "Look at you. Egad, you're even dressed. What time is it?"

"Eight-thirty." Gabby circled an ad for a vacant basement apartment in downtown Burbank and passed over another offering free room and board in exchange for "female companionship." One had to draw the line somewhere. "I need to get an early start this morning."

"It's Sunday," Samantha reminded her, peering over her shoulder at the newspaper. "No one gets an early start on Sunday. It's sacrilegious. What are you doing, anyway?"

"Starting over," Gabby said, dropping her forehead into her hands and frowning thoughtfully. "Samantha, what do you know about Santa Ysidro? Isn't it just south of here?"

"Yes, indeed. South of the *border*," Samantha qualified dryly. "As in Tijuana."

"Oh." Gabby grimaced and nibbled on the end of her marker. "No wonder apartments are so reasonable there. How about Blanding?"

Samantha dropped into a chair, regarding Gabby with something akin to horror. "It doesn't ring a bell," she said slowly. *"Blanding?* Why on earth would you want to move to a place called Blanding? My dear, towns are given certain names for very definite reasons. Blanding was probably derived from bland, as in ho-hum. It was most likely a toss-up between that and Blahville. Whatever happened to Laguna, Malibu, San Clemente, *civilization?"*

"Civilization," Gabby explained glumly, "costs. In my price range, I'll be fortunate to find something with indoor plumbing."

Samantha made a soft "ahem." Her Tootsie-Roll brown eyes were wide beneath ruffled bangs, like Tweetybird assessing a delicate situation. "Try as I might," she said finally, "I cannot think of a tactful way to say this. Does this decision of yours to 'start over' have anything to do with the wedding gown hanging in the front hall closet?"

Gabby doodled along the edge of the newspaper with her Valentine-red marker. With a start she read what she had written: *MikeMikeMikeMike . . .* "Alan," she said, quite loudly. "His name was Alan and he was going to make me the happiest woman on the earth. He said so. And it almost happened, only . . ."

"Only?" Samantha prompted softly. "What happened?"

"I'm not sure. Maybe the thought of all that happiness scared me." As she talked, Gabby's pen quickly turned the *Mike* scribbles into a huge red ink spot. Was there such a thing as a Freudian doodle? Mike had a nasty habit of creeping into her subconscious when she least expected him. This was no time for emotional detours, particularly when her life was crashing down around her ears. In the midst of an earthquake, one did not stop to smell the flowers. "I changed my mind at the last second, and everything has been going downhill since."

"Well, you've reached rock bottom if you're going to move to a place called Blanding, I'll tell you that." Samantha reached for an orange from the basket on the table and began peeling it methodically. "Which brings me to my next question. *Why* are you moving?"

"Because I *said* I was going to move. I gave up my lease." Gabby managed quite a cheerful smile, all things considered. "You should know that as well as anyone.

Our landlord is not one to let the grass grow under his feet."

"Exactly!" Samantha beamed and popped an orange segment into her mouth with a flourish. "*Our* landlord. As in you and me. Look, I don't want to interfere or anything, but as long as we're both here, why not take advantage of it? We can split the rent, which would be a godsend to both of us. Until I land another toothpaste commercial, I'm counting every dime. It doesn't have to be a permanent arrangement, but it would at least give you time to find a job before you look around for new digs. What do you say?"

"I don't know. I never considered..." Gabby stopped abruptly, a frown creasing her brow. "How did you know I was looking for a job?"

Samantha hesitated. "It was a calculated guess," she said reluctantly. "I know it's none of my business, but ... if you aren't in a financial crunch, I'll eat my Equity card. And since I'm in the same boat, we may as well keep each other company."

Gabby dutifully considered her options for the space of thirty seconds, quickly coming to the conclusion that there were no options to consider. Samantha was friendly, bright, and extremely easy to get along with. Despite her fragile appearance and breezy approach to life, Gabby sensed in her something of a soulmate, a survivor who was far stronger than she looked. Samantha's offer was indeed a godsend, a chance to stop and breathe and try to get her bearings.

"You're sure?" Gabby asked slowly. "I know you didn't plan on having a roommate..."

"I told you, you would be doing me a favor. We'll split everything down the middle, fifty-fifty. Is it a deal?"

"Deal." Gabby grinned and held out her hand, shaking Samantha's across the table. "You have no idea how relieved I am. I had visions of spending the nights on a park bench with a newspaper over my face."

"You see?" Samantha asked admiringly. "That would never have occurred to me, but what could be more logical? You probably know the Santa Ana Freeway like the back of your hand."

"There's a thought," Gabby said wryly. "Maybe I should apply for a position as a bus driver."

They were preparing a celebratory breakfast of blueberry blintzes—Gabby's diet having been temporarily postponed—when a light tattoo sounded at the front door. Gabby wiped her blueberry-tinted hands on the dishtowel tied around her waist and trailed Kitty to the door. She didn't bother looking through the peephole this time. The muscles contracting in her stomach and the quivery feelings in her chest heralded her guest's arrival.

"Your lips are purple," Mike said by way of greeting. He was wearing navy jogging shorts and a sweat-stained white tank top. A navy print bandanna was rolled and tied across his forehead, knotted at the back of his wind-tossed, rainbow-blond head. Sun-browned skin—a vast, *distracting* expanse of sun-browned skin—shimmered with perspiration in the hazy morning light. It was impossible to ignore the muscles that rippled like water wherever Gabby's eyes roamed. At least she was able to refrain from drooling. She still retained some small measure of control, no mean feat considering the movable feast before her. He's a terrible influence on me, Gabby thought. I never struggled with these lecherous tendencies when I was with Alan.

Gabby cleared her throat once, twice. "How kind of you to ask. I'm fine, thank you. And how are you this morning?"

"Thirsty," Mike replied, adding a blistering smile to Gabby's struggle. "Why are your lips purple, Irish?"

"Sam's making blueberry blintzes," Gabby explained, fixing her eyes on a neutral point in the middle of his chin. Better. "Would you like a drink? I've got juice or water or milk . . . and tea, I'm sure there's a pot of tea on—"

"Sam?" Mike leaned one hip against the doorjamb, crossing his arms over his chest. Golden eyes studied Gabby intently, analyzing, dissecting, categorizing. "And who is Sam?" he asked softly. "I hope I'm not interrupting anything."

Gabby had her mouth open to set him straight when Samantha came padding around the corner and into the living room, all legs and eyes and sleep-ruffled blond hair. Gabby glanced from Mike's spreading smile to her new roommate's slender curves, charmingly displayed in the pink nightshirt. The thin, filmy, clinging, extremely short pink nightshirt.

"I thought I heard a bass voice out here," Samantha said. She smiled at Mike, her brown eyes sparkling with undisguised curiosity. "Hello, there. I hope I'm not interrupting anything."

"*No one* is interrupting anything," Gabby snapped. Standing between a Greek god in athletic shorts and a wood nymph in a nightie, she suddenly felt a tad over-dressed. "Mike, I'd like you to meet Samantha Monroe, Mr. Paulsen's new tenant and my new roommate. Sam, this is Michael Hyatt, our neighbor down the beach."

"Oh, good." Samantha was fairly bubbling, and to-tally unselfconscious. If it bothered her to meet a perfect stranger half-dressed—or half-undressed, depending on one's point of view—she gave no sign of it. "Now I know where to go for a cup of sugar."

"You certainly do," Mike said cheerfully. He spared Gabby a brief glance. "Roommate? Does this mean you won't be thrown out into the streets after all?"

Gabby managed a tight little smile. Mike's concern for her well-being was positively underwhelming. "I guess not. Are you very disappointed? I know you were looking forward to getting rid of Kitty."

"Oh, I can still get rid of Kitty," Mike murmured. "Accidents will happen, you know. Samantha, it's very nice to meet you. Do you like cats?"

"Guilty, I'm afraid." Samantha chuckled, and the pink nightshirt slipped off one bare shoulder. Gabby resisted an urge to yank it back into place again.

"Ah, well," Mike sighed, "everyone can't be perfect. I'll forgive you that one small character deficiency be-cause you have chocolate-colored eyes. My favorite fla-vor," he added with a flash of white teeth.

He looked like a pirate, Gabby thought. A charming barbarian in search of high adventure, buried treasure, and fair maidens to ravish. Not to mention what he would do to an innocent cat. He had barely glanced in her direction since Samantha with the chocolate eyes had walked into the room. Gabby was alarmed to find herself feeling pitifully inadequate, a reject in the pirate game of pillage and plunder.

"Chocolate eyes?" Samantha repeated, a dimple dancing in and out of her cheek. "I think all this exercise is affecting your appetite, Michael."

"I'm starving," he admitted, "and my friends call me Mike. If we're going to be neighbors, we can't be formal. Ladies, I have a terrific idea. I think we should celebrate Samantha's arrival in our cat-infested community with a night on the town. You two can dress up in your Sunday best and I'll wear garters with my socks. Irish, you could wear your wedding dress. It would be a shame not to get a little use out of it. What do you say?"

"I say," Gabby bit out through clenched teeth, "that you can take your garters and—"

"Wear them," Samantha said hastily. "It sounds wonderful. We'll look forward to it."

Mike's eyes gleamed with amusement. "Will you?" he mused softly, holding Gabby's smoky-blue gaze. "Then it's settled. Seven o'clock tonight."

"In the meantime," Samantha put in smoothly, "why don't you join us for breakfast? I'm attempting blueberry blintzes, but if they don't turn out we have Pop-Tarts standing by on the side."

"Thanks, but I'll have to take a rain check." Mike raked a hand through sweat-dampened hair, grimacing ruefully. "I still have a few miles to put behind me before I reward myself with breakfast. You know, you ought to take up running, Irish. It would whip you into condition in no time at all."

"Exercise is painful," Gabby said with dignity. "If I ever get into masochism, I'll buy a pair of cleats and give you a call."

"Sounds kinky," he said approvingly. "Would you like to take in a movie after dinner tonight? They're showing *Meter Maids In Bondage* at the Rialto."

Samantha choked. Gabby whimpered and rolled her eyes to the ceiling.

"Another time, perhaps." Mike nodded understandingly. "I'll let you get back to your culinary efforts, ladies. See you tonight."

"What about your drink?" Gabby asked. "You said you were thirsty."

Mike turned in the doorway, soft creases bracketing his very best bone-melting smile. "I think I'll wait till I get home. Self-denial is an excellent way to build character."

"Do you practice it much?" Gabby murmured innocently. "Self-denial?"

"Since meeting you, Irish," Mike said pleasantly, "it's become a new way of life."

Chapter
5

GABBY NEVER PAUSED to question her motives. She dressed to kill, reassuring herself that it was entirely natural for a woman to want to look her best, whatever the occasion. The fact that Mike had seen her at her worst, both physically and emotionally, had no bearing on her decision to "gild the lily." None whatsoever.

The delicate silk midi-dress she donned had originally been intended for her honeymoon, the sort of dress one wore to walk on the beach beneath a lovers' moon. It was strapless and cut in a chic wrap-around design, the sky-blue material clinging like a cloud wherever it touched. It was also the sort of dress that would melt away by simply pulling the bow at the waist. Very practical for honeymoons, but a bit reckless for a night on the town with Mike and Samantha. Gabby tied the bow in a double knot and told herself it would be foolish not to get a little use out of her trousseau.

Whatever her motives, the end certainly justified the means. Mike arrived promptly at seven, lean and elegant in a charcoal-gray three-piece suit. He smiled easily at Samantha, complimenting her on the ruffled yellow sundress that set off her honey-gold tan. He turned to Gabby and the smile stuck on his face as if he suddenly had nowhere to put it. Golden eyes stretched, traveling the length of her figure, lingering at strategic points. Gabby fiddled with the knot at her waist, looped her hair behind her ears, shifted her weight from one foot to the other. When it appeared that Mike had forgotten his manners, she said huskily, "Good evening. You're right on time."

"Am I?" he asked, eyeing the rich fall of hair brushing her shoulders. After a moment's pause, he added a belated, "Good evening."

"You were right," Gabby went on, trying to fill a thick silence. "You *are* intimidating in a three-piece suit."

"Really?" He loosened his tie, his eyes tracing the roundness of her breasts for the second time. "Is that all there is?" he asked faintly.

Gabby blinked. "I beg your pardon?"

"The dress," Mike explained hastily. "Is that all there is of it? Don't you have a shawl or a sweater or something? Maybe a blouse you forgot to put on?"

"I don't believe this," Samantha murmured. "Now I have heard everything."

Mike threw her an irritated look and turned back to

Gabby. "I just thought you might want some sort of wrap. It's quite cool outside. I wouldn't want you to catch cold . . . not to mention the restaurant. I'm sure you'll want to throw something over your shoulders at the restaurant."

"I'll be fine," Gabby said stiffly. What was this? Three hours of primping, and Mike wanted to cover her up with a shawl? Samantha's dress, with its see-through bodice that revealed a low-cut teddy, was by far the more daring of the two. Why didn't he try to put a blouse on *her?* "Alan was with me when I bought this dress," she added, self-consciously smoothing the material over her hips. "He's very conservative, and *he* didn't have any objections. In fact, he picked it out."

"I haven't any objections," Mike muttered, yanking at his tie yet again. "Why should I object? You look beautiful, absolutely stunning. I just didn't want you to get cold. It was simple courtesy, that's all."

"Thoughtful of you, Mike." Samantha's warm brown eyes sparkled with amusement. "It's so refreshing to meet a man who still takes time to practice common courtesy. By the way, I don't believe I'll need a sweater, either. Just in case you were wondering."

"It was my next question," he said without expression. "Well, then, since neither of you feels the need for a sweater—and Lord knows I'm certainly warm enough— shall we go?"

The restaurant Mike chose was a favorite of the locals and the yachtsmen in the area. It was built of massive old timbers near the water's edge, a stone's throw from the docks where several small crafts were moored. The magic words, "Hyatt, reservation for three," produced a charming candlelit table on a rustic outdoor deck overlooking the sea. The decor was limited to colorful paper lanterns strung overhead, and the soothing sounds of water lapping against the pilings provided the only background music. The mouth-watering aroma of fresh seafood mingled with the salty Pacific breeze, piquing Gabby's appetite. She and Samantha perused their menus for fifteen minutes before Mike finally signaled the waitress and ordered for them, choosing a combination plate that offered a sample of nearly everything on the menu.

"Perfect." Samantha grinned, sipping at a pale-green fruity concoction thick with slivered ice. "I had it narrowed down to nine entrees and couldn't decide which to eliminate. This way I get a bit of everything and don't look like a glutton."

"I know what you mean," Gabby said feelingly. "I adore seafood. Clams, shrimp, lobster, oysters, crab . . . anything that once lived in the deep blue sea. I can't tell you how much I've missed it this past year."

Mike had seemed somewhat preoccupied, but at this his thick lashes swept up and his burnt-honey eyes focused on Gabby. "What's this?" he asked curiously. "Didn't Prince Alan share your fishy passion?"

"In a manner of speaking. He was terribly allergic to shellfish and made it a rule never to eat in a restaurant that specialized in seafood. He was always afraid something in the soup or side dishes would send him to the hospital." Gabby stirred her ginger ale with a pink-tipped finger. No alcohol tonight. It was simple good sense to keep a clear head when wearing a dress held together by a fragile blue ribbon. "I had to learn to like Mexican food. Alan never got tired of enchiladas."

Mike whistled through his teeth, eyebrows disappearing into his wind-tossed hair. "Can it be?" he asked, his voice warmly taunting. "A flaw in Prince Alan? A physical disorder?"

"He had an *allergy*," Gabby said irritably. "It wasn't his fault. Other than that, he was perfectly healthy."

"He may have seemed healthy," Mike countered wisely, "but this allergy could have been just the tip of the iceberg. Who knows what his condition could have led to? Seizures, indigestion, malnutrition, consumption, palsy, boils, carbuncles, eruptions—"

"Enough already." Samantha's eyes were huge in her pale face. "I can't believe you expect me to eat marinated herring after that. Mike, love, can't you talk about something pleasant?"

Mike smiled innocently, hands clasped before him on the table. "I was. Another drink, Sam?"

Mike, love. Sam. Gabby concentrated on her dinner and tried to ignore the friendly camaraderie Mike and Samantha had established almost instantly. There was something so natural, so spontaneous, about their lively exchanges that Gabby spent the better part of the evening feeling like excess baggage. It wasn't as if she was *ignored*, precisely; Mike more than fulfilled his duties as a host, and Samantha was her charming, disarming self. It was simply the fact that Samantha had dinner with *Mike, love,* and Gabby had dinner with Michael William Stanfield Hyatt II. Intimidating Michael Hyatt, in the three-piece suit. Irritating Michael Hyatt, who kept looking at Gabby's perfectly respectable dress as if it were made of Saran Wrap and tassels. Frustrating Michael Hyatt, who finally *insisted* Gabby was cold and forced her to wear his gray linen jacket over her shoulders. Gabby had begun the evening feeling like an attractive and desirable woman. By the time dessert was served, Mike had somehow reduced her to the status of an eccentric maiden aunt with weak lungs. It was not the effect Gabby was accustomed to having on the opposite sex, particularly when she had gone to so much trouble to look her best. There was a point of honor involved here. Mike had seen her depressed, soaked to the bone, bleeding from the feet, and running off at the mouth. He had seen her dressed in a tattered, filthy wedding gown and a threadbare antique sweatshirt. Feminine pride demanded that she at least try to redeem herself. How was she to know that Mike turned into a lunatic beneath a full moon?

Throughout the thirty-minute ride home, Gabby sat in brooding silence. She deliberately refrained from seconding Samantha's suggestion that Mike come in for coffee, for all the good it did. While Samantha puttered in the kitchen, Mike made himself right at home, pulling off his tie and flicking on the television. Gabby watched him from the shadows of her umbrella plant, one foot tapping silently on the rug. She still wore his jacket, not wanting to offend him with the sight of her—gasp!— *bare shoulders*.

Mike settled on an old Lon Chaney movie and dropped onto the couch, propping his feet on the coffee table. "This is great," he said conversationally, hooking his hands behind his neck. "Have you ever seen this movie?"

Gabby wondered if he could feel her eyes boring into the back of his head. "No."

"I used to watch *Chiller Theater* every Friday night. Vincent Price, Lon Chaney, Bella Lugosi . . . man, they don't make them like that anymore. Did you ever see *The Fly?*"

"No."

"Oh. What about *The Wax Museum?* Everybody saw that."

"I didn't."

"Oh." Mike glanced hesitantly over his shoulder. "I'm running out of meaningless conversation, Irish."

"Really?" Gabby pulled a dead leaf off her plant. It needed to be watered.

He cleared his throat and ventured cautiously, "Am I correct in assuming you are ticked off at me?"

Gabby raised her brows innocently. "Ticked off? As in upset? Not at all. I think I'll go help Sam with the coffee. Excuse me."

"Hold it right there." Mike grabbed her arm as she passed the couch. His jacket slipped to the floor in a gray puddle. "I can explain."

"There's no need to explain," Gabby bit out through clenched teeth, trying to free her arm. "None at all. You probably saved me from catching my death of a cold. Next time I'll wear my thermal underwear and save you the trouble."

"Michael William," he said resignedly.

"I beg your pardon?"

"Michael William," he repeated. "It's what my mother

called me when *she* was ticked off."

One quick tug and Gabby fell over the side of the couch and into Mike's arms. Her sandals flew through the air, landing with soft thumps on the carpet. Mike's arm was hard beneath her shoulders, pulling her against him. One hand moved to cup her face, brushing a drift of ebony hair from her forehead. He was close, so very close, and Gabby could smell the musky fragrance of his skin through his silk shirt. She saw herself in lazy golden eyes, an intimate self-portrait that held her spellbound. No doubt she should say something clever about being manhandled, but other than a rather theatrical "Release me, fiend," nothing came to mind.

"It gets to be something of a strain," he said softly.

Gabby frowned, making an effort to concentrate. "What does?"

"Watching men watching you." His hand drifted to her throat, a crooked smile shaping the firmly molded lips. "They did, you know. From cocktails to dessert, and there wasn't a damn thing I could do about it short of shoving you under the table. I never realized I had this dangerous streak of possessiveness until tonight. You ruined my whole evening, Irish."

"You could have fooled me," Gabby returned stiffly. Her skirt had ridden up beneath her hips, and the all-important blue ribbon was dangling over the edge of the couch. Strapless wrap-around dresses were not made for acrobatics. "You and Sam seemed to be getting along quite well."

"We did," he said. His lips brushed her temple, barely touching the delicate skin. "Sam is a very comfortable girl to be around."

"And I'm not?"

"Sweetheart"—his laughter was soft and faintly rueful—"I can honestly say that I have never been comfortable in your company. It's a situation I hope to remedy in the near future."

Lamplight loved his face, Gabby discovered. She was fascinated by the shadow play on his features, the smile that drifted slowly away from the erotic curve of his mouth. His face had taken on an intent, sleepy expression that left Gabby shaken and stripped of pretense. She tumbled deeper and deeper into glittering golden eyes, content for the moment to follow him.

Mike shifted his gaze to her mouth, dragging his thumb across her trembling lower lip. Gabby shook her head fractionally, denying... what? Calmly perverse, Mike smiled and nodded, sweeping aside her mute protest. He dipped his head, touching her lips with a sweetly probing sensuality. Gabby sighed against his mouth, a sigh that seemed to go on forever. She was home again, her senses reeling in the velvet-soft touch and unholy temptation of Mike's kiss. *Satan, get thee behind me ... but not yet. Oh, please, not yet.*

When Mike raised his head, his lips were honeyed from the moisture of the kiss and his eyes were soft and unfocused. "Nectar of Gabrielle," he whispered huskily. "How did I ever survive without it?"

Silence trembled between them, while Gabby tried to stem the hunger spilling within her. Hunger and something more, something so close to love that the breath caught in her throat with an odd, painful rattle.

A moment or two passed. Gabby stared blindly over Mike's shoulder, growing colder and colder with the despair that whispered over her nerve endings like a killing frost. Mike said something, tried to pull her closer. Instinctively, she pulled back, registering him in her heart with a bittersweet finality: the suddenly wary eyes, the muscle working in his cheek, the tiny, threadlike scar that cut across the cleft in his chin. Her eyes fastened on the scar as she acknowledged the old familiar apathy deadening her senses, dulling her emotions to a perfect blank. Probably a war wound from childhood battles, she thought absently, a schoolboy's badge of courage. He might have gotten it playing king of the hill or tumbling off a bicycle. She would never know.

Pots and pans clattered in the kitchen, Samantha's gentle hint that she was returning to the living room. Gabby slid off Mike's lap, smoothing her dress and refastening the belt. Her hands were perfectly steady, despite Mike's thoughtful gaze following her every movement. She bent and picked up his jacket, folding it carefully over the back of the sofa.

"This isn't going to work," he said at last. "You ought to know that by now."

Gabby's face didn't change. "I don't know what you mean. Your jacket's covered with cat hair from the rug. You'll have to have it cleaned."

"Thank you," he said politely. "I'll send you the bill. You know, you really shouldn't underestimate me, Irish. Play with fire if you like, but don't pretend you don't know what you're doing."

Samantha walked into the thick silence carrying a cookie sheet laden with coffee and cups. "Sorry I took so long," she greeted them cheerfully. "I couldn't find a tray, so I settled on a cookie sheet. I still have to learn my way around the kitchen. So! What have you two been up to?"

Chapter

6

IT WAS STENCILED in sunshine yellow on a plaque hanging in Gabby's kitchen—her motto, her creed, her tongue-in-cheek words of wisdom for all those who cared to read it: LIFE IS HARD...AND THEN YOU DIE. Gabby had first spotted the plaque at an art festival in Laguna Beach. It had appealed to her offbeat sense of humor and never failed to bring a smile to her face. Hopeless pessimism was somehow far more cheerful than eternal optimism.

Until today. Now Gabby sat woodenly at her kitchen table, staring at the sign that suddenly didn't seem quite so humorous. All things considered, she was getting the sinking feeling that her cute little plaque hit the nail right on the head. Life is hard and then you die... or if you aren't so fortunate, you go instead to your ex-fiancé's home and return your engagement ring.

Life could be worse, she reasoned glumly, although at this particular moment she couldn't imagine how. In the five days since her seafood extravaganza, Gabby had worn out two pairs of brand-new shoes in her futile search for a job. She had spent a small fortune in postage returning wedding gifts. She had spent a large fortune repairing a broken fuel pump on her Rabbit, not to mention the six hours she had spent stranded on the freeway when her car broke down. She had also met several interesting men riding the bus while her car was in the garage, including one sweet-faced old gentleman who invited her to join him for a soak in his hot tub.

Any normal person would take to her bed and refuse to get up again. Not Gabrielle Cates, no sirree. Thanks to a nagging conscience, *she* was going to top off this excellent week with a visit to Alan DeSpain's lovely home, wherein also dwelled Alan DeSpain's lovely mother. The selfsame woman who had persisted in calling Gabby *Miss Cates* during the first eight months of their acquaintance, the very same loving mother who fainted dead away when told of her son's engagement. Gabby could hardly wait.

And then there was Mike.

Gabby's mouth drooped along with her spirits as she thought of her golden-eyed neighbor. He had come over exactly twice in the last five days—once to borrow an egg, and once to return Kitty, who had somehow found his way into Mike's bedroom again. Both times Gabby had been home alone, and both times Mike had left as quickly as he had come. He was friendly, he was cheerful, and he made absolutely no effort to rekindle their earlier intimacy. A good neighbor, a fine friend, and a very painful thorn in Gabby's side. Not to mention the other tender parts of her anatomy.

For the first time in her life, her mind and her body seemed to have developed two separate and distinct personalities. Mentally, she was able to maintain a sensible and level-headed attitude, forcing Mike into a dusty little corner of her mind where he belonged. Physically, however, a stranger had come to town. A highly emotional stranger. A highly emotional stranger with an overactive libido. At least once a night Gabby woke up in a cold sweat with Mike's name on her lips. She had developed a healthy respect for a cold shower and a glass of warm milk with an occasional sleeping pill thrown in on the side. The circles under her eyes grew darker each night, and each morning the makeup covering them got heavier. Gabby swore off coffee, hoping to alleviate the restless anxiety that fueled her X-rated dreams. When that didn't help, she gave up chocolate, and when that didn't help she went back to all her nasty habits with a vengeance.

This morning she was breakfasting on Swiss Mocha coffee and chocolate-covered raisins. And as soon as the raisins were gone, she promised herself firmly, she would get this business of returning Alan's ring over and done with. That in itself could go a long way toward a good night's sleep.

Samantha stumbled into the kitchen, smothering a yawn and grimacing at Gabby's meal. "That's disgusting," she croaked, her voice still thick with sleep. "Hell's bells, raisins? Do you know what raisins are? Rancid grapes, that's what. And chocolate-covered, no less. Can I have some?"

Gabby grinned and handed her the box. "Be my guest. You could use a few calories."

"Not me, m'dear." Samantha slumped into a chair and tossed a handful of raisins into her mouth. "The camera adds ten pounds, you know. If I want to sell jeans, I'd better be able to get into them."

A few days earlier, Samantha had been selected to make a series of commercials for a famous brand of designer jeans. It wasn't Oscar material, she admitted ruefully, but it was definitely a step above toothpaste ads.

"I wouldn't worry about it." Gabby smiled. "You have the healthiest appetite of anyone I know, yet you never gain an ounce. It's revolting."

"Speaking of revolting, are you still determined to return that ring this morning? Why won't you take my advice and *send* it to him? Or better yet, sell the thing and buy yourself a new car."

Gabby took a deep breath and pushed herself away from the table. "No can do. I took the coward's way out at the wedding. The least I can do is return the ring in person."

"It's a mistake," Samantha prophesied darkly. "You're going to regret it. I feel it in my bones."

Gabby grabbed her keys and purse from the kitchen counter, grimacing at Samantha over her shoulder. "Thanks for the pep talk. I can't tell you how much better you've made me feel."

Samantha smiled and popped another raisin into her

mouth. "What else are friends for?"

Parking in Alan's circular driveway sixty minutes later, Gabby realized she should have paid more attention to Samantha's bones. The huge Tudor house that had once seemed so majestic had never looked colder or more forbidding. Alan's Mercedes was nowhere in sight, and the curtains were drawn over the gray-tinted windows. Perhaps Alan and Mrs. DeSpain had had such a lovely honeymoon—or rather, vacation—that they had decided to stay on in Maui. If so, Gabby would tell herself she tried and send the ring to Alan by special messenger. One should never look a gift horse in the mouth.

The massive front door swung open just as Gabby had her hand raised to knock.

"I saw you drive in," Mrs. DeSpain said coldly. "If you've come to see Alan, I'm afraid you're out of luck. He left first thing this morning for the office and told me not to expect him home until late this evening."

Damn, damn, and double damn. "Good morning, Mrs. DeSpain. How are you?"

The silver-haired woman raised one thinly penciled brow. "I'm sure you really don't want to know the answer to that," she sniffed, fingering the pearl necklace around her throat. "You made your feelings quite clear at the church, Gabrielle. Thank God Alan finally saw you for what you are. My sensibilities are of no importance. Alan comes first, despite the embarrassment and discomfort I suffered personally. Alan has always come first with me. Naturally, I don't expect you to understand that."

"I need to speak to Alan," Gabby said woodenly. "If you would please tell him I came by—"

"Come in, Gabrielle." Mrs. DeSpain pulled the door wide and retreated into the shadows.

"I really should be going..."

"Come in. I have something to say to you."

Gabby walked silently into the gloomy hallway, squinting in the half-light. She smelled lemon polish and the faint odor of bread baking, mingled with the cloying scent of too much Chanel No. 5. Mrs. DeSpain moved closer, and the Chanel moved with her. Germ warfare.

"I'm keeping you," Gabby said faintly. "I should have telephoned."

"I don't think so." Her cold green eyes raked Gabby's face. "I really don't think so. Your telephone calls would be just as unwelcome as your visits, Gabrielle. I'm sorry to be so blunt, but you're being quite...obtuse about all this."

"Really?" Gabby shrugged, two spots of color burning high on her cheeks. "I'm sorry. It must be terribly difficult for you."

"Sarcasm doesn't become you," the older woman snapped. "I can see I'm going to have to spell this out. I've been down on my knees giving thanks since you walked out on the wedding. Oh, Alan was disappointed, but he'll get over it. It was the lesser of two evils, and I'm sure he'll realize that someday. How he ever thought a person with your background could be a suitable wife and mother—"

"My background?" Gabby's head jerked up, her eyes wild. Her fingers curled into tight fists, nails digging into her palms. "What are you trying to say, Mrs. DeSpain?"

"It's quite simple. Did you really imagine you would

be a suitable wife for a DeSpain? A young woman of illegitimate birth, who has no idea who her father is? Good Lord, he could be anyone, *anything*. And your mother, such a devoted woman that she abandoned a five-year-old girl and never looked back? My dear, your own mother couldn't bring herself to accept you. Whatever made you think you were good enough for Alan?"

There wasn't enough air in her lungs to manage more than a faint rasp. "He said it didn't matter."

"What else was he supposed to say? If you'll remember, he had already asked you to marry him when you told him the truth. He was too honorable a man to withdraw his offer."

"He told you that?" Gabby began to shake, nausea slamming her in the stomach.

Mrs. DeSpain smiled serenely. "There was no need. I understand my son far better than a woman like you could ever hope to."

It took Gabby an eternity to get the ring off her finger. Her hands were stiff and clammy, refusing to respond to her desperate commands. She fumbled, and the ring slipped out of her fingers and dropped to the plush brown carpet. Gabby left it, not at all sure she could stand again if she knelt to retrieve it.

"You surprise me," Mrs. DeSpain murmured. "I assumed you would keep the ring. Payment for services rendered, or whatever you would call it."

Gabby stepped back, felt behind her for the doorknob. She felt ill, hot, simmering in ugly, destructive emotions. She managed to open the door and turned to face the sun, gulping fresh, pure air. When she spoke, she kept

her back to Alan's mother, and her voice was barely
audible. "When I think that she might have been a witch
like you . . . I'm glad. I'm glad she left."

Somehow Gabby made it to the car. Eyes wide and
distant, she started the engine and drove. She drove me-
chanically, braking for stoplights she never really saw,
following endless roads that led nowhere. She drove until
the midday sun was baking her little Rabbit, and the
sweat was trickling down the small of her back. She
drove until the gas gauge read Empty, and continued to
drive until the car began choking and spitting, rocking
to a halt on a quiet residential sidestreet. She became
aware of her surroundings gradually, noticing the modest
brick homes with red tile roofs, the wide, tree-lined streets,
the children who played kick-the-can in a shady side
yard. The street signs said Princeton and Highland Drive,
two names that were entirely unfamiliar to Gabby. Where
was she? Should she ask the children where the nearest
gas station was? Did it really matter?

She left the car unlocked and began to walk. She had
to keep moving. It was so much easier not to think if
she kept moving. She felt as if she were poised on the
edge of a cliff, teetering, knowing the slightest whisper
of wind would send her freefalling to the rocks below.
Memories kept surfacing, terrifying memories that were
as brilliant and painful today as they had been twenty-
odd years before. It seemed that time was not the great
healer after all. With a few brutal, well-chosen words,
Mrs. DeSpain had laid open the wound that seemed to
be eternally festering. And like so many times before,
Gabby bled.

She had been wearing a blue gingham ribbon in her hair. She still remembered that one detail, the ribbon she had tied herself with clumsy five-year-old fingers. She remembered standing at a dirty window, watching Momma back the car down the rutted gravel driveway. It seemed as if she stood at that window forever, until her stomach twisted with hunger and the sun slipped behind the wooded hills. And she remembered crying for her dinner, and wrapping herself in a worn baby quilt when the house grew dark and cold . . .

Gabby shivered. She was cold. The sun had set and the wind was rising, sweeping off the Pacific with a cold, damp sting. She couldn't see the ocean, but she could smell the salt air and hear the angry rumbling as the tide rolled in. The houses she walked by grew shabbier, the yards wild and neglected. Thirty minutes later, she realized she had left the run-down residential area behind. She seemed to be in some sort of an industrial park. She was surrounded by office buildings and warehouses, and tiny convenience stores seemed to light every corner. Without consciously making the decision, she closed herself in a lighted phone booth, fumbling through her purse until she found a quarter. She dialed the only number she could remember, her own.

Sam answered on the second ring. There was an odd catch in her voice, as if she had been running. "Yes? Hello?"

"Sam?" Gabby used her free hand to brush away the tears rolling down her cheeks. She wondered how long she'd been crying without knowing it. "Sam, it's me."

"*Gabby?* Where in the name of heaven are you? I've

been worried sick. You told me you'd be back at noon, and it's nearly midnight!"

Gabby swallowed over the aching knot in her throat. "Is it? It doesn't seem that dark. Maybe because of all the lights . . . everything's lit up here. All the parking lots, all the buildings. You can hardly tell the sun's gone down."

"Where are you? Gabby, are you all right?"

"I'm tired." Damn, she was crying again. The tears were blurring her vision, spilling like rain onto the black plastic receiver. Damn Momma. Damn Mrs. DeSpain. Damn the juvenile delinquent who stuck bubble gum all over the floor of the telephone booth. "I'm not sure where I am. I ran out of gas. I can't remember where I left the car . . ."

There was a brief silence at the other end of the line. When Samantha spoke again, her voice was soft and deliberate. "I'm going to come and get you, Gabby. Tell me where you are and I'll be right there."

"I don't *know.*" Now Gabby was sobbing, clutching the phone with white-knuckled fingers. "Some kind of store. It says . . . DAY-NIGHT MARKET. I'm so tired, Sam."

"Gabby . . . what happened? Are you hurt?"

Gabby watched a patrol car drive past, momentarily blinded by the sweeping headlights. "You were right. I shouldn't have gone to see Alan. If I hadn't gone to see him, none of it would have happened."

"Look for a street sign," Samantha said. "Tell me what it says."

"Kemmer." Gabby's voice was unutterably weary. "It just says Kemmer."

"Stay there, Gabby. Wait inside the store."

The line went dead.

Gabby drifted across the deserted parking lot and into the store. She bought a cup of coffee and tried to ignore the curious eyes of the attendant at the cash register. He looked wary, as if he imagined she might pull out a gun at any moment and demand all his money. Did she look like a thief? She could just imagine the description he would give the police . . . a strange-looking woman who walked out of nowhere, splotchy face, horribly swollen eyes. *Her heart wasn't in her work, officer. She kept crying and crying . . .*

Gabby pretended a great interest in the gossip tabloids displayed near the front counter, then moved to the magazine racks and thumbed blindly through *Dirt Bike Quarterly*. Over the top of the magazine, she saw the powerful black Porsche turn into the parking lot, recognized the broad-shouldered figure practically leaping from the car. His hair looked wild, as if he'd been lost in a windstorm, and his face was set in stone. St. Michael to the rescue once again, savior of cats and broken-hearted ladies . . .

She dropped the magazine and went into his arms like a lost and frightened child. Just being *held* . . . it was all she wanted, it was all she had ever wanted.

"It's all right," Mike said quietly, his breath stirring the tendrils of hair at her temple. "I'm here, Gabby. I'm taking you home."

"Sam—"

"She called me. I had a fairly good idea where you were, despite your lousy directions. Next time try to be a little more specific, Irish."

"I'm sorry." She wasn't. She clung to him with desperate hands, not bothering to conceal the emotion in her bruised eyes. She knew with a sudden flash of insight that Mike was the one she had wanted all along. She hadn't been waiting for Samantha at all. She was simply too tired now to pretend.

Keeping her within the circle of his arms, he led her to the car, tucking her in the passenger side with gentle hands. He said nothing until they had turned circles on a clover-leaf and entered the freeway. He was driving slower than usual, glancing over at Gabby every few minutes. "Sam told me you went to see Alan," he said finally. "Do you want to talk about it?"

Gabby shook her head mutely, closing her eyes against the memories. She quickly opened them again, because it was worse to be in the dark. "Can we turn on the radio? I'd like to hear some music."

Mike's hand closed over hers as she reached for the stereo. "Not yet. Tell me what happened, Irish. I have to know. I nearly went out of my mind after Sam called me. As a matter of fact, if you don't start talking soon, it's still a possibility."

"Mike?"

His eyes met hers, glittering with emotions held tightly in check. Then he looked back at the freeway, his features blurred in the yellow light from the instrument panel. "What?"

"Take me home with you."

He sat very still, looking straight ahead. His hair fell in a bright tangle over his forehead, softening the harsh profile. "I'm no hero," he said quietly. "If you're looking for comfort, love . . . you'd do better to look somewhere else."

"Not comfort." Gabby shook her head faintly, trying to find the words. She felt light-headed, strange, and she realized with something like despair that she was lost without him tonight. "Not comfort . . . just an hour or two without having to think."

"Oblivion? Is that what you want, then?" Something clicked over in his features, a change reflected in the light that strangled in his eyes and the skin that whitened and stretched over taut cheekbones. He looked like a man in pain, Gabby thought, staring at him through a haze of confusion. Was the whole world in pain tonight?

"Why not?" she whispered dully. She sensed the change in him, something new and undefinable, but inexplicably a barrier. To her tired mind and the body that seemed one giant nerve ending, it was yet another rejection. "No past, no future, no questions to be asked or answered. I think that's what heaven must be like."

"Funny." Mike slanted her a bittersweet smile that ended almost before it began. "It sounds like hell to me."

"Mike—"

"Close your eyes," he said. "Rest. We'll be home soon."

Gabby pulled the drapes in Mike's living room, staring out at the dark void that was the ocean. He placed a sweater over her shoulders, something warm and fuzzy that reached nearly to her knees, and went to the kitchen to call Samantha. Their conversation was brief; it seemed only seconds later that he returned, pressing a glass of something into Gabby's stiff fingers.

"What is it?" she asked, not really caring.

"Something to warm you up," he said quietly. "You're shaking like a leaf."

Gabby frowned, looking down at the drink she held. The liquid shimmered with a fiery glow, tossing from side to side in the glass and dripping through her fingers. "I didn't realize. I'm not cold. I don't know why I'm shaking."

"Don't you?"

She met his eyes, her own brilliant with unshed tears. Her lips were dry and hot, and she moistened them with her tongue. "You don't want me here, do you?"

Something flared in his eyes, but was quickly banked. "Drink," he said flatly, turning away. "I'll see if the guest room is ready."

"Why didn't you take me home?" she whispered, her voice cracking embarrassingly on the last word.

He was staring off into nothing, his hands pushed in his pockets, a beautiful cold stranger who seemed a million miles away. Gabby waited until she decided he had no intention of answering. She twisted back to the window and gulped her drink, feeling the liquor flow like molten lava down her throat. Although she stood back to back with Mike, she could still see his reflection in the opaque glass. She watched him turn his head until his profile was etched in lamplight, her eyes caught and held by the shining mass of wheat-blond hair. Michelangelo's "David" in Levi Strauss.

"I wanted to keep an eye on you," he said suddenly. "I didn't think you should be alone, I thought you might need a friend, I was worried about you . . . choose one or all of the above. It doesn't really matter, because I'm a damn liar. You're here because you wanted me tonight, and I thought that would be enough."

"But it isn't?" Gabby felt an odd, sharp pain writhe deep inside, knowing she had hurt him.

"You said it yourself, Irish. You want oblivion. I want *you*. That kind of puts me at a disadvantage, don't you think?"

She watched his reflection in the window until he had disappeared up the stairs leading to the second floor. She set her drink on the nearby grand piano, thought of water rings, and picked it back up again. By the time she took it into the kitchen and returned to the living room, Mike was descending the stairs again.

"Both the extra bedrooms are made up," he said. "You can have your pick. I'll have to give my housekeeper a raise for her foresight."

"Mike," Gabby began hesitantly, "I think it would be better if you took me home—"

"What? And miss this opportunity to demonstrate my remarkable self-control?" Above his smile his eyes were stark, expressionless. "I wouldn't hear of it. Besides, my Porsche has been tucked into bed for the night. Now follow me and we'll try to do this thing as painlessly as possible."

"What thing?" Gabby asked automatically, following his shadow up the stairs. A part of her recognized the inner desperation under the play, but she had no idea how to deal with it.

"Saying good night," he responded, nodding at the

first door at the top of the stairs. "Now say good night, Irish."

Don't go. Please don't go. "Good night."

He swung on his heel, taking the stairs three at a time. Gabby stood silently in the hallway until she heard an ice bucket rattling, then turned and went into the bedroom. She barely noticed the exquisite white on white decor, nor was she conscious that she had left the bedroom door wide open. She walked straight to the bed and, sitting gingerly on the edge of a shimmering silk spread, wiggled her feet until her shoes dropped off. Soft white light spilled from a lamp on the nightstand, casting a pearly, translucent glow over the bed while the rest of the room slept in shadows. Gabby stretched back at an angle, supporting herself on her elbows, and closed her eyes. Any moment now she would find the energy to hang up her clothes and slide between the sheets. Any moment now.

When she opened her eyes again, Mike was standing in front of her. His eyes had changed color since she last saw him. They seemed to be the most intense source of light in the room, a dazzling molten-gold, soul-deep and unguarded.

"I could have done it," he said, "if you hadn't left the damn door open."

Gabby pushed herself upright, clasping her trembling hands in her lap. "Done what?"

"Walked past your room. Slept alone in my own bed. *Controlled myself.*"

"And now?" Gabby whispered. Considering the lack of oxygen in her lungs, it was amazing she could make any sound at all.

"And now"—Mike's hands closed over her wrists and he pulled her to her feet—"all bets are off. You, my sweet, blue-eyed angel, cheated."

The husky, slightly ragged edge to his voice, the hard flush on his cheekbones, the pulse slamming at the base of his throat, all drew hungry, deep-rooted responses from Gabby's senses. In all her lifetime, she had never wanted anyone or anything as much as she wanted Michael now. She knew suddenly why she had left the bedroom door open, why she had waited on the beautiful four-poster bed like an anxious child. It wasn't possible to want something this badly and not get it. In between the nightmares, there were still dreams, dreams that could become reality.

Mike's arms curved around her waist, drawing her closer. He buried his face in her hair, kissing the soft ebony strands over and over. Gabby whispered his name, watching with hot indigo eyes as he pulled back slightly, hands lifting in slow motion to frame her feverish face.

"I can give you so much more than oblivion," he said huskily, dipping his head toward her. "Give me a chance, Irish. Let me ... give ..." He seemed to lose interest in the words as his mouth closed over hers. Gentle kisses of lazily altering pressure warmed and softened and molded her lips, until Gabby's mouth was a ring of searing fire. Seized by need, she moved against him, one palm sliding restlessly over his back, the other seeking his neck, her fingers digging into the silken hair. She felt drugged, half-crazed, her body arched in the narcotic cradle of his hips.

Mike's hands burned their way down her back, grasping her buttocks and thrusting her closer still. Hands, hips, thighs increased their hungry rocking motions until Gabby was blind with need. Kisses that had begun as controlled, tempting promises grew mindless, almost primitive, tongue strokes carrying the physical motion of love. Gabby's greed to know more of him seemed to know no bounds; she reveled in the roughness of his cheek, the hardness of his teeth, the wetness of his mouth. Her entire existence was centered on this moment, every raw nerve in her body attuned to this man. Sweet oblivion. How could he give her more than this?

He broke from her, sex-flushed, golden eyes liquid and unfocused. Gabby lifted heavy black lashes to stare at him, her mouth shining wetly in the soft light. Her breath came in shallow, erratic exhalations, leaving her light-headed and drifting.

"I've waited"—Mike's hands slipped over her arms, fingers closing on the narrow straps of her sundress—"so long." Clumsily, he slipped the dress off her shoulders, holding her gaze while it floated to the carpet in a shimmer of pale-blue fabric. Gabby's eyes closed, and her head lolled back on her neck as his hands slid downward to lift and caress her breasts. She felt her nipples, engorged and pulsing, straining against the white silk camisole she wore.

His mouth covered hers, swallowing her hoarse cry of pleasure as his thumbs rubbed erotically across her nipples through the feather-light fabric. Gabby melted against him, hands clutching convulsively at the front of his shirt. Dragging reluctantly over the moistness of her lips, Mike trailed swirling kisses over blood-hot cheeks, caressed the pulse shimmering with sweat at the base of her throat, fastened finally, instinctively, on the rose-hued crests in their filmy covering. The gentle suckling left Gabby weak and aching, the wet white silk only adding to the flood of sensation.

When Mike raised his head, the rush of air on the damp fabric spread in velvet shimmers through her breasts. Gabby whispered his name, astonished at the unknown nerves he had activated, showers of color and heat she'd never experienced before. When she thought her legs could no longer support her, Mike read her mind, lifting her in gentle arms and laying her crosswise on the bed. Gabby's body stretched tantalizingly, silk against silk, her eyes tangled helplessly with his. Her own name was lost to her, but she knew every restless movement of his body, every sigh, every pulse. And she knew the hunger he felt, because it was her own, burning her from the inside out.

Still caught in her eyes, Mike shed his clothes, everything dropping in a heap on the floor. He joined her in one fluid motion, tucking her body beneath him and adding his warmth to skin already blistering with heat. Gabby's head turned mindlessly from side to side, and when his hands removed the last barrier of clothing, her shaking fingers impatiently assisted him. He whispered something against her mouth, repeating the words over and over, words that Gabby lost in the heat of her desire. Her hands lifted and cradled his face, seeking and caressing the beautifully symmetrical features. Mike connected with her eyes in a dazed, softly preoccupied way, his hands memorizing every curve and valley of her flesh until Gabby was shivering with reaction. Her nails dug into the sweat-dampened skin of his back, something deep and primitive stirring within her.

"Mike," she murmured thickly. "Mike, I need..."

"Say it, Irish." His voice was unsteady, blurred with passion. "Say 'I need you.' *Say it.*"

"I need you." It came easily in that sexually charged moment. Had he commanded her to fly, Gabby thought dreamily, it would have come just as easily.

She saw his eyes darken with an expression she couldn't fathom, saw him smile tenderly, softly down at her as he entered her, scattering the last remnants of coherent thought. Strong hands caught and held her hips as he eased himself deeper, and deeper still. They danced to an ancient rhythm, moving in perfect unison of mind and body. Lost in a brilliant void of sensation, Gabby clung fast to her only reality: Mike's eyes. Beneath love-tossed golden hair, they burned into Gabby's soul, keeping her with him until her sweet oblivion became too much to bear. Then, and only then, did Gabby understand. Mike gave her dreams, dreams that flowed unselfishly through him to her. Dreams, she discovered, drowning in the sun-shot colors of his eyes, that he shared.

The lamp was still burning when Gabby awoke.

Dawn filtered through the drapes, frosting the tumbled white bedcovers. She opened her eyes in time to see the lamp flicker, hiccup quietly, and die. She knew without turning that Mike lay beside her, although her back was curved away from him. A touch, a whisper, and it would all begin again.

Yet Gabby lay still, rigid, paralyzed, while her mind

tried desperately to sort fantasy from reality. Dear Lord
. . . had he actually said he loved her?

She remembered now, with the blinding, agonizing
clarity that comes when emotion is spent. Mike's voice,
murmuring over and over against her open mouth: *I love
you, I love you, I love you . . .*

She took a deep, deep breath and held it. Then she
let it go, past the aching knot in her throat. She turned
her head fractionally on the pillow, until her eyes caught
the soft glow of disheveled blond hair. Scene by scene,
she recalled the night before, committing it to memory.
Then, soundlessly, she rose, gathering her clothes and
shoes and taking them into the bathroom, where she
dressed. Better to go now than later, when he might
convince her to stay. More than likely his declaration of
love had been spontaneous, the kindness of a friend who
had seen her through the night. For Mike's sake, she
hoped so. She was done with using people, done with
false security and broken promises. She had given him
all she was capable of, all she knew how to give.

She paused at the doorway, memorizing one final scene.
Mike asleep, unguarded, shimmering through a haze of
tears. Another breach of "morning after" etiquette—slipping away at the break of dawn while the gentleman lay
sleeping. Perhaps now Mike would understand. The lady
wasn't worth the effort.

Chapter
7

ONCE HOME, GABBY removed her shoes and tried to tiptoe into her room without waking Samantha. She felt rather like a guilty husband sneaking home after a night of carousing. She wasn't up to any long explanations, particularly when she hadn't yet been able to explain last night's events to herself. *Events*. What a horrible word, making the time spent with Mike sound like a special category in the Olympics. It hadn't been like that at all. It had been wonderful, magic, healing. She knew all the moments in her life from now on would have to be measured against those few short hours in Mike's arms.

But how to explain that to anyone else? Particularly when she had no intention of ever letting it happen again.

She was stealing past the kitchen doorway when Samantha spotted her.

"There you are," Sam crowed, jumping up from the kitchen table and pointing an accusing finger. "You little devil, you. I want to hear everything, from the beginning to the end. Well, not *everything*. You can leave out the extremely personal stuff, and I'll fill in the blanks with my colorful imagination. I'm very creative."

Gabby dropped her shoes on the linoleum with a clatter. "I don't know what you're talking about," she said faintly. "I didn't think you'd be up this early."

"You mean you *hoped* I wouldn't be up. Not a chance, m'dear. When you didn't come home last night, I set my alarm for five o'clock. I've gone through four tea bags since then."

Samantha's childlike enthusiasm was impossible to resist. Gabby found herself smiling, despite the fact that there was absolutely nothing to smile about. "You idiot. You set your alarm just so you could check up on me?"

"Not *check* up," Samantha corrected. *"Keep* up. There's a difference, you know. Watching you go through life is like watching a soap opera twenty-four hours a day. I can't wait to see what happens next. Last night was the cliffhanger, leaving me chewing on my nails and worrying myself sick. Hopefully, this morning you will tell me that all has been resolved. Has it?"

Gabby busied herself poking around in the refrigerator for some breakfast she didn't really want. "I'm sorry you were worried," she said evasively, smelling a half-empty carton of yogurt. "Look at this, my very own home-grown polio vaccine . . . didn't Mike call you? He said he was going to."

"Oh, he called all right. He told me you were in sad shape and he was going to look after you."

"I was," Gabby mumbled. "And he did." *Boy, did he ever*.

"I knew it! I could tell by the way he watched you when we went out to dinner that the man had ulterior motives." Samantha beamed, giving Gabby and the banana she had found one swift, hard hug. "You don't have to thank me, really. All I did was give the two of you a little push in the right direction. You did the rest."

Gabby avoided Samantha's eyes, making a great production out of peeling the banana. "And what makes you think anything happened?"

"You have to be kidding," Samantha drawled. "It's written all over your face, kiddo. You have the look of someone who's had very little sleep and doesn't mind at all."

"Do *you* mind?" Gabby heard herself ask. "I mean, you and Mike..."

Samantha blinked. "Mike and I what?"

"You're so comfortable together. I thought maybe you might have some ideas in that direction yourself."

Samantha suddenly choked, thumping herself several times on the chest before she caught her breath once again. "Excuse me," she gasped weakly. "Something caught in my throat. Gabby, I think Mike is one of the nicest men I've ever met. I really do. I just don't happen to be ... you know, *romantically* attracted to him. You know how it is, either it clicks with someone or it doesn't."

"I don't see how anyone could avoid clicking around him," Gabby mumbled through her banana. She was anything but pleased at this pronouncement, and Samantha regarded her with a puzzled frown.

"So why aren't we smiling?" Samantha asked finally. "There *is* life after Alan DeSpain. Last night was a small step for womankind, but a giant leap for Gabrielle Cates. Why aren't we celebrating this lovely development?"

Gabby closed her eyes, massaging a dull ache at the back of her neck. "Because we're confused," she said tiredly. "Samantha, please don't make more out of this than there is. I was feeling pretty low last night. I don't want to get into it all now, but suffice it to say that my visit to Alan's home was not a roaring success. When Mike found me, all I wanted was a shoulder to cry on. That's the story in a nutshell, pure and simple."

"A shoulder to cry on?" Samantha asked blankly. "You said you *clicked.*"

"Of course we clicked!" Gabby replied irritably. "The man could wring a response from a loaf of bread. That doesn't change the facts." Her voice had risen to something resembling a wail.

Gabby forced herself to take a steadying breath before continuing. "The last thing in the world I need right now is another involvement, with Michael Hyatt or anyone else. Last night was ... well, last night. Two ships passing in the night, a port in the storm, a moment out of time." *What a muddle.* "I'm going to take a shower now, and then crawl back into bed for a few hours. If Mike calls, tell him..."

"Tell him what?" Samantha prompted quietly.

Gabby visualized him waking up in an empty bed, an empty house. "Never mind," she whispered dully. "I don't think I'll be hearing from him."

* * *

Had it been any other day but Saturday, Gabby might have managed to get through it with some semblance of dignity. Unfortunately, advertising agencies were closed on Saturday, and she couldn't work out her frustrations pounding the pavement looking for a job. After tossing and turning in her bed for forty-five minutes, she abandoned the idea of catching up on her sleep. She dressed in jeans and a cotton middy top, and killed three hours watching *Celebrity Bowling* and *American Bandstand*. Samantha was in and out of the house all morning, sunning herself down on the beach, whipping up a batch of oatmeal cookies, and reciting dialogue for an audition to Kitty on the front steps.

Despite her conviction that Mike was going to want nothing to do with her after her little vanishing act— hadn't he already explained the proper etiquette for The Morning After?—Gabby was a bundle of raw nerves. Every time the telephone rang she jumped a mile, and whenever Samantha opened the front door she cringed, half-afraid that Mike would be standing there with fire in his eyes. Finally, she decided to escape in her Rabbit for a drive up the coast, only to recall she had abandoned the car miles away.

After scanning Sam's bus map and miraculously finding Princeton and Highland Drive on it, she left the house for the bus stop, waited only a few moments for the bus, and then boarded it, happy that luck seemed to be back on her side. Once in the sought-after neighborhood, she purchased a two-gallon jug of gasoline, asked directions, then began the long hike in search of her car, getting lost only twice. By the time she had emptied the last drop of fuel into her tank, she was covered with grease and had blisters on her hands the size of walnuts, effectively neutralizing any sense of accomplishment she might have had. Gabby didn't give a damn what the women's movement proclaimed. Self-reliance was not everything it was cracked up to be.

The ten o'clock news came and went that evening before Gabby finally realized that Mike was not going to come storming after her. She shut herself into a room with a Sara Lee cheesecake and told herself it was all for the best. However he might feel about her now, at least she had managed to face her own limitations. Love was something that happened to other people, while Gabrielle the dreamer stood back and watched through a cold plate-glass window. She could pretend and fantasize, even fool herself now and then, but reality was always just one step behind. She took no risks, and that gave her safety, peace . . . and loneliness. It was the price she had to pay to protect the little girl inside the woman. A small price, considering the alternatives. She had had enough pain and disappointment to last a lifetime.

The cheesecake was only a memory when Samantha burst through the bedroom door with a panic-stricken expression and an armful of sopping-wet towels. "You've got to help me," she wailed, glancing over her shoulder as if she expected to see Count Dracula in pursuit. "I don't know what happened, I swear I don't! All I did was *flush* the thing! Gabby, it's pouring into the hall and I can't get it to stop. Do you know where any more towels are?"

"What on earth are you talking about?" Gabby asked slowly. "Sam, those towels are dripping all over the carpet."

"Dripping towels are the least of my worries," Sam snapped. "I can't swim, and if I don't find a way to stop our toilet from overflowing, I am going to meet a very nasty end. *Where are the dry towels?*"

Gabby vaulted off the bed, landing in her stocking feet in a half-inch of water. A steady stream was flowing down the hall from the bathroom in waves. "Why didn't you say so?" she yelped, springing across the spongelike carpet. "Pull the dirty towels out of the hamper and block off the bathroom door. I'll try to turn off the water."

Gabby waded into the bathroom, appalled at the sight that met her eyes. The yellowed linoleum was completely submerged under three inches of rust-colored water, water that was streaming into the rest of the house despite Samantha's efforts to dam off the doorway. The toilet was making an ominous rumbling, spewing forth water like some sort of unique indoor fountain. Gabby tried desperately to turn the valves behind the tank, with no success. She grabbed a hairbrush and tried using it as a lever to force the valves to turn. The hairbrush broke into pieces and the water continued to bubble into the house.

"I've used every towel I can find," Samantha said breathlessly. "The living room is under water. The cat is on top of the fridge. I thought he would be safer there. Oh, and I called the nearest plumber."

Gabby stared at her rather blankly for a moment, then tugged her already sopping pants above her knees and sloshed into the hallway. "The plumber," she said, focusing on the one point in Samantha's speech that seemed relevant. "What did he say? When can he get here?"

"First thing in the morning," Samantha replied miserably. "Ten o'clock at the latest."

"We'll be washed out to sea by then," Gabby muttered. "Look, there has to be a main shut-off valve somewhere. We'll just have to find it and turn off the water to the whole house. You look in the kitchen and I'll check around outside. Oh, Lordy, Mr. Paulsen is going to *kill* us."

After ten minutes, neither Samantha nor Gabby had been successful in locating the main valve. The water flooding the house was ankle-deep and rising. Gabby did manage to disconnect the cords to the major appliances, with some vague idea of avoiding death by electrocution.

"What about another plumber?" Gabby suggested, blinking back the tears that threatened to overflow. More moisture would not improve the situation. "Couldn't we try calling someone else?"

Samantha watched a rubber thong float slowly down the hall and sniffed. "It's nearly midnight. Even if we found someone who would come out at this time of night, who knows how long it would take him to . . . to . . . Mike!"

Gabby jumped. "Where?"

"Why didn't I think of him before?" Samantha demanded. She hitched up her skirt and splashed down the hall, glancing at Gabby over her shoulder. "I'll call him with an SOS. He's a man, he *has* to know how to turn the water off."

As reluctant as Gabby was to face Mike again, she could hardly argue with Samantha's plan. They were clearly up the creek with no paddle—an interesting expression—and had nowhere else to turn.

Seconds later, Samantha was back. "He's coming,"

she announced. "He made all kinds of noises about spigots and septic tanks, so I assume he knows what he's doing. Smile, my friend, the cavalry is on its way."

"Oh, good," Gabby said flatly. Butterflies took flight in her stomach, winging their way into her throat. She busied herself bailing water out the bathroom window, desperately wishing that her scattered wits would come together and suggest the proper way of handling the coming encounter. What to say to the man who had taken you to heaven and back the night before, the same man you had run out on without a word of explanation . . . and who was now on his way to do battle with your sewage system?

What indeed?

It seemed only seconds later that Mike was there, filling up the bathroom doorway and turning the tiny room into a steambath with his smile. He was wearing a yellow crewneck sweater and faded blue jeans rolled up to his knees. His hair was lightly tousled and his gemstone eyes softened with amusement. Gabby drank him in for perhaps five seconds of spine-tingling pleasure before another gurgle from the plumbing brought her tumbling back to reality.

"Hi there," he greeted her amiably. "What's a nice girl like you doing—"

"Oh, *please*." Samantha peered over Mike's shoulder from the hallway. "Can't we save the bathroom humor for another time? We have a crisis situation here, Mike. Do you know where the shut-off valve for the water is?"

"Nope." He raised a hand and patted Samantha's golden head reassuringly. "But I'll find it. Don't give up the ship, ladies. Rescue is at hand." And he walked down the hallway whistling "Anchors Aweigh."

Gabby leaned tiredly against the wall, holding a Tupperware bucket in one hand and a three-hundred-pound, soaking-wet velour towel in the other. The man confounded her right and left. Where was the anger, the hostility? It had been impossible to detect even the slightest hint of the rejected lover in his demeanor. Tonight he had metamorphosed into Mr. Rogers of the seashore, friendly neighbor and all-around swell guy. If he even remembered the young lady he had made passionate love to the evening before, he gave no sign of it. Gabby raised bewildered eyes and found Samantha frowning at her across the Red Sea.

"You don't look at all well," Samantha observed thoughtfully. "Not at all. Is something wrong?"

Gabby's fingers gave up their fight with the wet towel. It dropped into the water swirling around her ankles, settling like an anchor over her feet. "You've got to be kidding," she said flatly. "Is anything *wrong?* Look around you and repeat that question with a straight face. I dare you."

"Oh, it's not that bad. How much damage can a little water do?"

"'A little water,'" Gabby echoed faintly. She sat down on the edge of the bathtub, dangling the bucket between her legs. "This is not 'a little water.' This is a flood. Have you any idea what it's going to cost to clean up this mess? And knowing Mr. Paulsen, he'll probably sue us into the bargain."

"It was an accident," Samantha said indignantly. "He

can't sue us because the plumbing went haywire . . . can he? Isn't that called an act of God, or something?"

"Who knows? I'm sure that whatever happens, it will all be for the worst. It's getting to be a pattern these days."

At that moment, the pipes began to vibrate beneath the floor, gurgling and choking, then suddenly falling silent. The water streaming from the toilet to the floor dwindled to a trickle, then ceased altogether with a tiny gasp.

"Hallelujah," Samantha breathed fervently. "He did it. Now do you think we can talk him into wielding a mop and a pail?"

"I wouldn't count on it," Gabby murmured uncomfortably. But Samantha was already gone, wading down the hall in search of her quarry. Gabby sighed and gathered up the mounds of wet towels, tossing them into the bathtub. She had absolutely no idea how to go about cleaning up this mess, but if Samantha thought a mop and pail would do the trick, she was in for a nasty shock.

She found Mike and Samantha sitting on the kitchen counter, sharing the available space with a toaster, a blender, and a disgruntled gray cat. Gabby's eyes traveled down to Mike's lean, muscled calves, thickly covered with dark brown hair. His feet were stained a pale pink from the rusty water, as were Samantha's. Gabby caught herself admiring the graceful line of his arches, wondering why the human foot was so undervalued. Despite the unnatural color, Mike's were really quite attractive. *Your self-control is pathetic, Gabrielle.*

"We're caucusing," Samantha announced glumly.

"Would you care to join us?"

Gabby looked at the minute counter space between Mike's thigh and the refrigerator. "I don't think so. I'm all wet."

Mike glanced down at his pants, the sopping denim clinging like a second skin. "Lord, no," he said. His eyes danced, the corner of a grin playing with his lips. "Don't get me wet. Which do you want first, Irish? The good news or the bad?"

"You mean there *is* good news?" Gabby asked in a small voice. She trained her eyes on Mike's hand resting on the counter, his fingers lightly tapping out a gentle rhythm. She knew only too well the wonderful relationship his body had with rhythm.

"Let me put it this way." He qualified his statement. "Things could be worse. Pumping the water out of here is going to be the least of your problems. The carpets are going to have to be replaced, along with some of the linoleum. Someone is going to have to come in and plaster and paint the walls again, not to mention the damage done to the furniture. When you girls do a job, you don't do it halfway. I don't think a hurricane could have equaled your little plumbing disaster."

"Is this the good news," Gabby asked weakly, "or the bad?"

"Patience, sweet. I've just been telling Sam that your landlord's renters' insurance will pay for the damages. Good news. Unfortunately, it could take several days to make the place habitable again. Bad news."

Samantha and Gabby regarded each other for a long moment, sighing in weary unison. "Do you recall that idea of yours about the park benches?" Samantha asked finally. "Now that I think about it, it might be fun. Plenty of fresh air, all sorts of interesting people to meet—"

"I hardly think it will come to that." Mike slid off the counter, grimacing as he hit the wet floor. He was all business, a figure of authority with red feet and water-logged jeans. "You're coming home with me, ladies."

"Oh, no we aren't." The words escaped before Gabby could stop them, panic rattling her voice. Immediately, two pairs of eyes swung in her direction, one startled, the other amused. Gabby swallowed hard, amending her blunt refusal to an unconvincing, "Thank you so much, but we couldn't impose."

"Oh, I insist," Mike replied, deadpan. "You have no idea how lonely it can get in that big house all by myself. I'll enjoy the company, and you two lovely ladies won't have to displace some poor transient from his park bench. That was the plan, wasn't it?"

"It was a joke," Gabby said hoarsely. "We can find a hotel room for the time being. We can stay at the YMCA. There are all sorts of solutions without putting you out."

"The YWCA," Mike said kindly.

"What?"

"The YWCA. You said the YMCA, which I'm sure must have been a slip of the tongue. A self-respecting young lady like yourself would never consider—"

"You know what I mean," Gabby snapped, turning to Samantha for support. "Tell him, Sam. Tell him we wouldn't dream of imposing like that."

"We wouldn't dream of imposing," Sam said dutifully, *"ordinarily.* However, considering the current state of my checkbook—and may I suggest that my roommate consider the current state of hers—we would be happy to accept your kind offer. Just until the cottage is cleaned up, of course."

"Of course." Mike's expression was nothing short of saintly. He held out a hand, assisting Samantha from her perch on the drain with courtly deference. "A wise decision, my lady. Gabrielle?"

"What?" Even to her own ears, Gabby sounded like a sulky child. Mike's offer was cloaked in kindness and buttoned up neatly with the best intentions, but it would have taken a signed deposition from God to make her trust him. Early on in their acquaintance, he had informed her he was not a good Samaritan, and she had no reason to believe he had experienced a sudden change of heart.

"Are you coming home with me?" he asked, his tone light, innocent, his smile dazzling.

Oh, Grandma, Gabby thought, *what sharp teeth you have* . . . "You make it difficult to refuse," she said.

"Say thank you, Irish."

"Thank you, Irish." None too warmly.

"I think you're tired," he said. "Well, it's no wonder you're a little irritable. All this nasty water, and then you were up so late last night . . . well, we won't talk about that. Is there anything I can do to help you pack?"

"Why, yes," Gabby replied, borrowing Mike's sweetly angelic smile. "You can be in charge of the litter box."

Fate, they say, loves a challenge. Once again Gabby found herself in the elegant white on white bedroom she had walked out of forever that very morning. It rendered her emotional exit from Michael Hyatt's life slightly anticlimactic, and left her feeling like a little white mouse on a treadmill. For all her efforts, she was right back where she started.

A breeze floated through the open window, billowing the floor-length curtains and giving Gabby's goosebumps baby goosebumps. She climbed out of bed yet again, closing the window she had opened fifteen minutes before. Obviously, fresh air was not the cure for insomnia.

Back to bed again. Pound the pillows, kick at the covers, listen to the tiny little snores coming from the adjoining bedroom and envy Samantha her untroubled sleep. How long had it been since Mike-The-Perfect-Gentleman had shown them to their rooms, pointed out his own door across the hall, and asked them to wake him if they needed anything? The bedside clock indicated a scant sixty minutes had passed, although it seemed much longer. Long enough for Samantha to shower and stick foam-rubber curlers into her hair before drifting off to dreamland. Long enough for Gabby to soak her aching muscles in a hot bath and turn the queen-size bed into something resembling a war zone. Long enough to remember how very different the night before had been.

Gabby flicked on the bedside radio, then turned it off again when the slow, sensuous music evoked the very mood she was trying to escape. She was cold, so she exchanged the pink silk pajamas she wore for a thick flannel granny gown that buttoned from waist to neck. She was hot, and the granny gown joined the pajamas on the floor. She finally settled on a soft white T-shirt, crawling back into bed just seconds before the bedroom door swung wide.

"You make more noise," he said softly, "than a herd of elephants."

Gabby gaped dumbly at him, pulling the covers to her chin. The light from the hallway outlined his silhouette, leaving his face in shadow. She knew, somehow, that he wasn't smiling.

"Is there anything I can get for you?" he asked politely. He walked into the room, closing the door behind him with his foot. "How about a glass of warm milk?" Closer, and even in the darkness she could see the bare chest rippling with lovely, tough muscles, the dark blur of pajama bottoms riding low on lean hips. Gabby felt her throat contract involuntarily, and she swallowed a gulp with raw determination.

"I'm just fine," she said, making an attempt at a normal voice and almost succeeding. *"Very* comfortable. Thank you."

"Are you quite sure there isn't another drawer or window you'd like to slam before we call it a night?"

Gabby wiggled deeper into the bed, giving him an excellent view of the top of her head. "I'm sorry. I'll try not to disturb you."

"Thank you, but it wouldn't make much difference whether you were trying or not." He sat down on the edge of the bed, drawing up one long leg and resting his chin on his knee. "You are a natural disturbance, sweetheart, like a tornado or an earthquake. Would you like me to tuck you into bed?"

"No."

"Plump up your pillows?"

"For heaven's sake, Mike—"

"I'm only trying to look after you. Have you got insomnia tonight, hmm?" He smiled, as if nothing would please him more.

"I *never* get insomnia," Gabby said coldly.

"Then why all the tossing and turning? It's two in the morning, and every good little girl with a clear conscience should be fast asleep. Just listen to Samantha . . . *such* a clear conscience."

"There is nothing wrong with my conscience!" Gabby flared. Cornered, she launched a full-scale attack on his luxurious guest accommodations. "It's freezing in here with the window open, and stifling with it shut! The bed is lumpy and the sheets keep falling off and I can hear a faucet dripping in the bathroom!"

"Strange," Mike murmured, holding her in his silken gaze, "you seemed so satisfied last night."

Checkmate. Gabby turned her head away, chewing viciously on her lower lip. The air around her steamed, and she looked longingly at the closed window.

"All right," Mike said softly. "Shall we get this over with?"

"Get what over with?" Gabby asked warily, glancing sideways at him through a heavy fringe of lashes. "I don't know what you're talking about."

"Thou shalt not lie," he chastised solemnly, one hand grasping her wrist and pulling her toward him. "You've been palpitating all night, waiting for me to pounce, so why don't we put you out of your misery? I, for one, would like to get some sleep tonight."

Gabby felt the heat of his body coming closer and put out a hand to push him away that somehow got tangled in his honey-blond hair. His mouth hovered over hers, caressing her lips with a sigh before he brought them slowly, slowly together. Passive as a dreamer, Gabby twisted into him, her heart turning over and over with the sweetness of his body pressing against hers. Her hands slipped over his shoulders, lovingly tracing the muscles cording his back, pulling him closer. She felt him shift his weight, hips pushing hips into the bed, and whirled in a warm, dizzy darkness. The worn cotton shirt that separated his body from hers did nothing to stem the growing desperation that caused her to arch against him.

When he suddenly raised his head, grasping her shoulders and pushing away from her, Gabby stared at him blindly, one fist pressed against her mouth. His pulse was a trip-hammer in his throat, the only indication of what his withdrawal might have cost.

"End of my brutal sexual advances," he said evenly. "Now you can relax for the rest of your visit."

Gabby's eyes were a deep, deep blue, and she flinched when Mike brushed a stray curl from her blood-hot cheek. "Don't," she whispered hoarsely. "Just . . . don't."

"I won't, love." Mike rose from the bed, leaving a musky, erotic fragrance still clinging to the sheets. "It's going to have to come from you this time. My neck's been on the chopping block long enough."

"What?" Her voice was less than a whisper, and Mike gave no indication of having heard. She repeated again, quite loudly, *"What?"* catching him at the bedroom door.

"It's your move," he said patiently. "Strangely enough, Irish, I don't want anything you aren't willing to give.

Oh, it would be fun while it lasted, but then you would have to go through another one of those dramatic early-morning escapes of yours. This way, you won't have to worry about it." He opened the door, giving Gabby a bittersweet smile that would live forever in her dreams. "Good night, love. If you ever decide to join the living, you know where to find me."

Chapter

8

THE DAWN BROUGHT mixed blessings. Finally, Gabby
was able to roll out of bed and call an end to the most
frustrating and exhausting night of her entire life. It was
a record-breaking low in an already hellish forty-eight
hours, giving a whole new meaning to the word *restless*.
Mike had left her in a bed that had suddenly taken on
the proportions of a football field, and a room that echoed
with emptiness. She could hardly recognize herself in
the confusion of mind and body that he had created. It
was impossible to separate one emotion from the next,
one sensation from the other. She was being punished,
she had been given a reprieve. She was hot and sticky
with frustration, she was shivering with cold despair. She
was angry, wistful, frightened, bewildered, lonely. She

was denied even the simple relief of thrashing about in bed or pacing the floor until sheer exhaustion overtook her. Mike's room was directly across the hall and she was determined not to give him the satisfaction of knowing she had passed a less than restful night. Muscles rigid, she lay for hours in dark misery, a prisoner of demon pride. She counted sheep, kittens, heartbeats, anything to fill the endless hours.

And when the sunrise finally put an end to the longest night in history, Gabby still had one more hurdle to face. Mike. Somewhere in his big, beautiful house he was waiting for her, armed to the teeth with his God-given sexual weapons. In the battle of the sexes, Michael Hyatt was a Green Beret. He also seemed to know exactly what he wanted, an advantage Gabby had lost the first time she looked into his eyes.

Cunning. The coming encounter called for a cunning mind and keen strategy. Mike could charm the angels out of heaven if he set his mind to it, let alone one insignificant young woman with a fatal weakness for honey-colored eyes. However appealing the man was, and however potent the sexual chemistry between them, Michael Hyatt would never be for her. There was no future in it for either of them.

Gabby dressed in the least attractive outfit she had brought with her, a drab brown jumpsuit that lent a yellowish tinge to her olive complexion. Her hair was pulled back in a schoolmarm bun and she deliberately left her face free of makeup. The result was nothing short of frumpsville, as Samantha confirmed when Gabby met her in the kitchen for breakfast. Thus far the enemy had not been sighted.

"You probably have a very good reason for looking as if you just escaped from *The Little House on the Prairie,*" Sam said kindly. "I can't wait to hear it. You know, I never noticed before how large your ears were."

"Then let us hope," Gabby replied serenely, "that our host has an aversion to large ears. Would you pass the milk, please?"

"Certainly." Samantha smiled with exaggerated politeness and pushed the white plastic jug across the table. "Cornflakes?"

"Please."

"Sugar?"

"Yes, thank you."

Leaving her own breakfast half-finished, Samantha chewed on a fingernail and studied Gabby thoughtfully. "Don't tell me," she said suddenly. "You're trying to discourage Mike's advances with that potato sack you're wearing. And the hair ... the hair is wonderful. What a nice touch. It's just a shame that Mike isn't here to appreciate it."

Gabby forced herself to swallow a spoonful of cereal before asking casually, "Oh? Where is he?"

"He left about thirty minutes ago, just as I came downstairs. He was going for his Sunday morning run on the beach. He said that we were to make ourselves completely at home and to please keep Kitty off the Oriental carpet."

"That's all?" Gabby felt curiously let down, as if she had given a war and no one had come. Also slightly ridiculous. "Did he say when he'd be back?"

"Nope. I suppose we'll see him when we see him. Does it really matter?"

If she hadn't known better, Gabby would have sworn he had left simply to irritate her. *Ah-ha, I'll let her dress up in her ugly stepsister disguise and then I'll slip out the back door. It'll drive her crazy.* "Of course it doesn't matter. I just thought it was a little strange that he would disappear like that when he has houseguests."

"We aren't houseguests," Sam said. "We're refugees. Mike was very kind to let us stay here, and you know it. We can't expect him to entertain us night and day."

"I don't," Gabby replied, stung. "If you'll remember, I was the one who objected to coming here in the first place. No one will be happier than yours truly when we can move back to the cottage. And speaking of which, as much as I'm dreading it, we ought to contact Mr. Paulsen this morning and tell him what happened. We'll need to contact his insurance company about the repairs."

"All taken care of." Samantha stood up and stretched, glancing around the spacious kitchen with obvious pleasure. "Mike got all the information this morning. The contractors will be on the job first thing tomorrow. Now, how shall I spend the rest of this lovely, lazy Sunday? Did you know Mike has a sauna in the master bath? I think I'll go down to the beach for an hour of sun, give my hair a hot-oil treatment, visit the sauna...I think I've died and gone to heaven. What are your plans today?"

"Evasive action."

"Evasive what?"

"Never mind." Gabby sighed. "It's a little complicated." Her new hairdo was stretching her scalp until her cheekbones ached, the hairpins digging like thorns. What's more, the nubby brown fabric of the jumpsuit was chafing like a burlap bag. Without an appreciative audience, her disguise was hardly worth the discomfort it caused. "You know, it's actually quite warm today. I believe I'll go and change into something less . . . less . . ."

"Repulsive?" Samantha suggested sweetly. She raised a hand above her head, pulling twice on an imaginary bell. "Ding-ding. At the end of round one, the score is Mike-one, Gabby-zero. Don't go away, sports fans. The excitement is just beginning."

As it turned out, round two was temporarily postponed. Throughout the remainder of the day, Mike gave his reluctant refugee lessons from a professional in evasive strategy. When Gabby was inside reading the Sunday paper, he was outside changing the oil in his Porsche. When Gabby went down to the beach for a swim, he went inside to take a shower. And when Gabby and Samantha sat down to a dinner of cold cuts and fresh fruit, Mike took a fishing pole, tacklebox, and plastic lawn chair down to the beach for a couple of hours of surf-fishing. Later, when the three of them shared a nightcap together, he was polite, amusing, and friendly, without crossing the line to intimacy. The looks he gave Gabby were no warmer than the looks he gave Samantha, and only slightly warmer than the looks he gave Kitty. Obviously, he was going to be a perfect gentleman. Gabby went up to bed with a tension headache and a glass of warm milk.

Her alarm went off at six-thirty the following morning. Gabby took a quick shower and dressed in her official career woman's black linen suit and white silk blouse.

She had a promising job interview scheduled, plus lunch at noon with Alicia. Add to that a visit to the dry cleaners, an afternoon matinee, and a visit to the gas station to have her flat tire repaired, and she ought to be able to kill an entire day without once being avoided. Far better to be the avoider than the avoidee, a lesson she had learned at her mother's knee.

She had gone to the kitchen for a quick cup of coffee when she spotted the yellow slip of paper under a magnetic mushroom on the refrigerator. Although she had never seen Mike's handwriting before, she recognized it immediately. Bold, forceful, and, yes, irritating. He didn't bother to dot his i's.

Sorry, pretty ladies—business emergency in Los Angeles. Mi casa es su casa. *Sammy, don't fall asleep in the sauna, you'll fry. I'll be back by Wednesday or Thursday.* NO CATS ALLOWED IN MY BEDROOM.

Foiled again. Gabby shut Kitty in Mike's bedroom without a litter box, then headed off to her job interview in a less than pleasant frame of mind. She had become so accustomed to everything in her life going wrong that she nearly fainted when the personnel director of Tanner & Tanner Advertising hired her on the spot. It would mean a sizable increase in salary from her last position, excellent benefits, and three—count them, three—weeks of paid vacation every year. Even the news that Gabby would not begin her new job for ten days couldn't dampen her rising spirits. Could it be that fate had found someone else to play nasty tricks on for a while?

Gabby felt her newfound security deserved some sort of celebration. She splurged that evening, taking home a full-course Chinese dinner for two in little white cartons. If Samantha had already eaten, she would just have to eat again.

The first thing she noticed when she entered the kitchen was the pink slip of paper which had joined Mike's under the magnetic mushroom. She put her cartons on the table and walked slowly to the refrigerator, squinting to read Samantha's baby-fine scrawl.

Agent called, foul-up in scheduling the jeans commercial. We're shooting in San Francisco tomorrow morning. Didn't want to leave without saying good-bye, so . . . good-bye! P.S. Be back in a couple of days or when you see me, whichever comes first. P.P.S. I let Kitty out of Mike's bedroom. Shame on you.

First Mike, then Samantha. Gabby shivered, feeling the enormous house echo hollowly around her. It could get awfully lonely during the next few days. All alone in a seaside palace with only Kitty for company. Funny how a person's likes and dislikes could change so quickly. Once upon a time, she had preferred her solitary existence in her little cottage. Now the thought of being alone was almost frightening.

She shared her sweet 'n' sour chicken with Kitty and fed the rest of the meal to the disposal. Something had happened to her appetite, and she no longer felt like celebrating. It wasn't much fun alone.

She left the kitchen spotless and wandered into the

living room. It was too quiet. She played her entire rep-
ertoire—which began and ended with "Chopsticks"—
on Mike's grand piano. Television was useless—the
President was smiling on every channel, giving the State
of Something address. Gabby wasn't feeling particularly
patriotic tonight, just . . . lonely.

She made a half-hearted attempt at sleeping. After
five minutes of lying in the dark with her eyelids glued
open, she thought of Mike's sauna. She reached for her
robe, then realized modesty was entirely unnecessary.
She could run naked through the house screaming if she
felt the urge. Kitty was very open-minded about things
like that.

Mike's bedroom was twice as large as her own, a
moody study in blues and browns, soft white lighting
accenting painting and bookcases. Gabby avoided looking at the bed with the same determination she avoided
hot fudge sundaes when she was dieting. Bare feet, bare
legs, bare everything, she padded across the room, toes
digging into the ultra-plush carpet. The sauna adjoined
the bathroom, a redwood paneled room with smoky blue
spotlights trained on the lava rock garden in the center.
Gabby stretched out on the redwood bench circling the
rock garden, feeling every muscle in her body quivering,
warming, and saying, "Ahh . . ."

She remembered Mike's warning about falling asleep
and set the built-in timer on the wall. When it rang, she
was on the edge of sleep, heat-flushed and shimmering
with perspiration. She barely had the energy to open the
sauna door, but the feeling was wonderful. If Mike were
here, he could touch her and mold her hot, Silly Putty
flesh into any shape he desired . . .

Out of the corner of her eye, she saw the blue silk dress shirt tossed carelessly over Mike's bed. She picked it up, feeling the smooth fabric clinging to her damp skin as she slipped it on. The cuffs fell several inches below her fingertips, and the shirttails barely covered the tops of her thighs. Excellent. Fastening only two of the buttons and feeling deliciously wicked, she went downstairs for a cold glass of ice water. Ice water, hell. She would have Scotch on the rocks.

It was two stiff drinks and another rousing rendition of "Chopsticks" later when she saw him. She was sitting on the piano bench, the slick hardwood cool against her bare bottom. He had silently materialized in the middle of the living room, complete with a cat chewing on his shoelaces. But it wasn't just *any* cat, Gabby realized happily. It was her own, her very dear Kitty.

"Sweet Kitty," she crooned, holding out one slightly tingling hand. "Come to Momma, precious. Here, Kitty, Kitty, Kitty... Hi, Mike."

"Hello." The one husky word barely moved his rigid mouth. He was in a suit, although not a *three*-piece suit, and he didn't look at all intimidating with his shirt halfway unbuttoned and his tie slung over his shoulder. He looked tired, a bit sloppy, and in need of a shave, but not intimidating.

"Well, this is a surprise." Giving up on her cat, who refused to give up on Mike's shoelaces, Gabby stood. She wasn't drunk, but she was certainly relaxed. As a matter of fact, she hadn't felt this relaxed since ... since ... for a long time. She smoothed Mike's shirt down over her hips and carefully buttoned every single button, from top to bottom. She had one left over at the neck, but there was nothing she could do about that now. "I didn't expect you back tonight. This is just a little bit embarrassing."

"Samantha," Mike said quietly.

"No . . . Gabby." Silly man. Had he been drinking, too?

"Where is she?"

"Oh. Didn't you read her note? It's under the muth— the mushroom. She had to go to San Francisco to shoot a commercial. She won't be back until we see her."

Silence. Gabby watched as Mike absorbed the information, blanched as he said slowly, "I am going to wring her little neck."

Relaxed though she might be, Gabby thought his reaction was unnecessarily harsh. And not at all like Mike, she realized with some misgiving. "Is it this shirt?" she asked apprehensively. "I'm sorry, really. The house seemed so empty and quiet with everyone gone. I couldn't sleep, so I used the sauna . . . the shirt was just *there*, on your bed, so I put it on. An empty house does not a modest woman make. Am I babbling?"

"Like a brook."

"I thought so." Gabby ducked her head, hiding behind a swirling cloud of blue-black hair. Concentrate. "Mike?"

"Hmm?"

"What are you doing here? You said you wouldn't be back until Wednesday or Thursday."

"I'll tell you in the morning. Right now you're going to bed."

Their eyes met, clashed across the room. "Am I?" Gabby whispered. It wasn't the alcohol talking, although she would have loved to shift the blame and pretend it was. Had she imbibed just a little more, she could have walked straight into his arms and not been held responsible for her actions. As it was, she could only look at him, trying to control the hot waves rippling over her skin. "I'm not really sleepy. Maybe we could play a game of cards or something..."

His response came quick as a slap. "Unless you get your fanny upstairs, it will be a game of *or something*. And we both know that isn't what you want...don't we?"

Gabby kept dry lips pressed firmly shut. She moved toward Mike, stooped to pick up Kitty, drifted up the stairs. It occurred to her as she entered the bedroom that one should never ascend a stairway dressed in one's birthday suit and a flapping shirt. However, Mike probably didn't even look. He was being so noble, so honorable. So irritating.

She opened the bedroom window, sat in a white rocker with quilted cushions, and listened to the ocean. She heard Mike coming up the stairs, heard the sharp click of his bedroom door closing. Something crashed against something else and Gabby heard a muffled curse. She smiled and waited ten more minutes before walking across the hall and tapping softly on his door. "Mike? Are you asleep?"

Another curse, this time softer and far more inventive. "What now?"

"I heard something."

"What?"

"I don't know. *Something*. I think someone's downstairs. Would you open this door, please?"

The door flew open, thudding against the wall. Mike stood before her in all his natural glory, plus one pair of soft cotton jeans he hadn't bothered to zip up. His golden eyes were underlined with dark circles, and Gabby realized he hadn't been sleeping any better the last few days than she had. Her confidence increased.

"What did you hear?" he bit out. He stood with legs slightly parted, hands on hips. With his surly, little-boy expression, Gabby half expected him to mark an imaginary line on the floor and dare her to cross it.

"I don't know what it was. Maybe it was just the wind, but I think you should go and check it out."

He smiled, and it wasn't a nice smile. "You go. If you find a burglar, sic your kitty on him."

"Mike, I'll never be able to sleep if you don't—"

"Hopping *hell*." He nearly mowed her down striding toward the stairs. Gabby waited until she heard him checking the doors in the kitchen, then she wandered into his room. The lights were a bit too bright. Something would have to be done about them right away. She found a dimmer switch on the wall and reduced Mike's electricity bill by half. That was much better.

His expensive clothes were strewn about the floor like damp bathtowels. His tie hung over a lampshade. One shoe lay on the carpet near the bed, the other was nowhere to be seen. Gabby smiled at the wreckage and sat down on a leather-cushioned window seat to wait.

Mike checked at the doorway when he saw her. He was a beautiful portrait of grim masculinity. He had managed to do up his zipper in the interim, although the snap at the waistband still gaped open. "There's no one down there," he said. "But then, you knew that, didn't you?"

Gabby rolled up the cuffs on his shirt until she had hands again. "I *hoped* there wasn't," she said, shrugging. "Still, you never know what you will find in your house at night."

"Especially your bedroom."

"I expect you mean me." Gabby's eyes were clear and untroubled, if a bit glazed. The moderate amount of alcohol she had consumed was just enough to heighten her appreciation of her surroundings without dulling her senses. At the moment, she was completely absorbed in appreciating Mike's incredibly sexy body. What was it about faded jeans and a bare chest that could turn a highly principled woman into a wanton hussy? Let alone a highly *unprincipled* woman.

"I expect I do," Mike said tightly. For a moment, his gaze dropped to Gabby's golden-brown legs, tantalizingly bare beneath his own silk shirt. He closed his eyes briefly, then focused on the butter-colored moon suspended in the window above her head. "I'm going to count to three. When I finish, I want you out of here. Gone. Invisible. Elsewhere. Is that clear?"

"Yes."

"One . . ."

"I hate it when people count."

"Two . . ."

"I came to return your shirt." Gabby stood, one hand going up to the buttons on the shirt. She smiled in pretty apology. "I should have never borrowed it without asking. I'm so sorry."

"Touch one more button," Mike said softly, "and I

swear I'll put you over my knee and spank the living daylights out of you."

"Barbarian," Gabby said, her tone serene. "Where did you learn that—*Meter Maids In Bondage?*" She finished unbuttoning the shirt quickly, before he could reach her. Still she remained more or less covered, until his hands closed over her shoulders with intent to kill. It was a tactical error. Gabby felt a rush of cool air on her over-heated skin, teasing the turgid points of her breasts, whispering over the delicate planes of her ribs, stomach, and hips. She was only vaguely aware of Mike's fingers clenching and unclenching, moving almost reluctantly over her collarbone, up to her neck where they lingered on the sensitive hollow pulsing with her lifeblood.

"Are you going to strangle me?" she whispered huskily.

"It's a possibility." The lines of stress around his mouth seemed to soften as he looked into the unguarded blue of her eyes. "Later."

Gabby stretched out a tentative finger, tracing an imaginary heart on his chest, skipping over to tease a hardened male nipple. "Later?" Her face nuzzled the golden-brown skin, her tongue replacing the stroking movements of her finger.

His stomach muscles contracted harshly. The hands that pulled the shirt off her shoulders were less than gentle, sending it flying across the room to join the tie on the rocking lampshade. "You asked for this, Delilah. Remember that."

"I didn't ask." Gabby's tremulous laugh caught in her throat as he swung her into his arms. "I begged."

"Irish, you don't know the meaning of the word." He lowered her to the bed, pinning her to the sheets with eyes that could have melted cold lead. "But you will. You will."

The faint smell of smoke roused her hours later. Too drowsy to feel alarmed, she gazed at the flickering red glow in the window seat where once the moon had hung. As her eyes adjusted to the darkness, the outline of Mike's body came into focus, one hand moving slowly to his mouth as he put the cigarette to his lips.

"Mike?"

He turned his head, looking at her through wispy spirals of smoke. "Go back to sleep, Irish."

There was something in his voice that brought her fully into consciousness. Something that frightened her. She slid off the bed, pulling the giant-size spread with her and wrapping it around her shoulders. Was it her imagination, or did Mike tense as she knelt before him on the carpet? "I didn't know you smoked," she whispered.

"I don't." He took another long drag on the cigarette. "I quit last year."

"Then..." Gabby frowned, freeing one hand from the folds of the bedspread and laying it cautiously on his thigh. There was no mistaking it. The muscles beneath her palm were rock-hard, pulsing with some unknown tension. "Why are you smoking now?"

He shrugged, turning back to the window. "It's an old habit I thought I'd broken. When I was under a lot of pressure with business, a cigarette seemed to help. Of course, everyone told me that was just my excuse for continuing a bad habit." He shifted on the window seat with a lazy grace, giving a faint smile to the darkness beyond. "Thank heaven I kept a spare pack around to test my willpower."

"Mike," Gabby murmured unevenly, "you're frightening me. What's wrong with you?"

He seemed not to hear. He continued to look out the window, golden eyes gleaming like candles in the night. "It's never been like that before," he said suddenly. "Never. You hold heaven and hell in the palm of your hand, Irish. It was almost worth it."

Gabby shivered, although she wasn't cold. "What was?"

"Loving you one more time," he said simply. "It was almost worth the look I'm going to see in your eyes tomorrow."

"What look?"

"Regret." His smile found her in the darkness, quite gentle. "I'm not kicking, Gabrielle. I knew what I was doing. I don't seem to have a hell of a lot of control where you're concerned, do I? I'm sorry."

"Sorry?" Gabby tried to cudgel her brain into coherence. "Mike, I don't understand."

"You will," he said. "In the morning, when all the old fears come back to haunt you. *Commitment*. You'll turn yourself inside out trying to find excuses for your behavior, and you won't have far to look. You had too much to drink, you were lonely, I took advantage of you. And you'll be right. Hell, it's probably beginning already, isn't it, love?"

"Is that what you think?" Softly. "You're wrong, Mike."

"Am I?" He crushed the cigarette against the windowsill. "I don't think so."

"Listen to me." Gabby frowned, trying to concentrate all her efforts on her words. She hardly noticed when the bedspread slid to her waist in a quilted blue cloud. "Tonight . . . tonight I knew exactly what I was doing. I wasn't drunk, and I'm not sorry."

"Maybe not yet." His voice seemed to come from far away. "Things may look different in the morning."

"I can see," she said very softly, "that I'm going to have to convince you. A woman's work is never done."

"Gabby, I'm not asking for—"

She shut him off with a hand over his mouth. "I don't want you to *ask*," she said, with all the innocence of a fallen angel. Still kneeling, she moved closer, smiling when his breath stopped on a ragged inhalation. "I want you to beg. You know what they say about love and war."

"All's fair?" His voice was hardly more than a hoarse whisper, and the hands that moved over Gabby's hair trembled. "Somehow I don't think they meant . . . this."

"Would you like me to stop?"

"No."

"Are you begging?"

"Yes . . . oh, yes . . ."

Chapter

9

"I'M NOT GOING TO touch you until noon."

Gabby bit into a piece of crisp bacon, eyeing Mike with interest across the table. "Really? Why not, pray tell?"

He leaned back in his chair and smiled, a delicious morning-after smile that touched Gabby like a caress. "It's a point of honor. You are constantly coming between me and my best intentions. I have to prove to myself that I can control my baser instincts. Do you have any idea what you did to me yesterday?"

Gabby dropped her chin into her palms, the sleeves of Mike's shirt fluttering down around her elbows on the table. It really was amazingly comfortable, far more so than her own robe. She planned on keeping it forever, along with his slippers. "Of course I remember what I did to you yesterday," she murmured languorously. "I remember every single wonderful, wicked, depraved . . . wasn't there a song called 'Love On The Rug'?"

"'Love On The Rocks,' Irish."

"Mike . . . are you blushing?"

"No. Men don't blush. I meant *yesterday,* not last night. When I was in Los Angeles."

"Your business emergency?"

"I lied. I was removing myself from temptation. I was determined that the next move would come from you, even if it killed me. And it nearly did. I ran myself ragged trying to avoid you on Sunday. Finally, I decided to drive back to L.A. and lose myself in business until you came to your senses."

Gabby raised one delicate brow. "Until I *what?*"

"Came to your senses," he repeated solemnly. "Admitted your passionate desire, begged for mercy, that sort of thing. You know."

"Uh-huh. So what happened?" Gabby lifted one bare foot under the table, finding Mike's thigh beneath the short brown toweling robe he wore.

"By the end of the day—*stop* that—by the end of the day, I had half my employees threatening to quit, my poor secretary in tears, and my vice-president begging me to go back on vacation. I was *not* in a good mood. All I could think about was the blue-eyed witch named Gabrielle who'd made me forget every high-minded principle my sainted mother instilled in me."

"Well!" Gabby's eyes flashed and she sat at attention.

"If you're trying to blame *me*—"

"Quiet. I'm on a roll. I was afraid if I stayed in Los Angeles one more day, I'd run my business into the ground. Rather than take that chance, I came back here . . . which was the only place in the world I really wanted to be." This time the smile he gave her was new, uncertain around the edges and somehow vulnerable. Gabby wondered if he had a treasure chest of smiles, a new one for every occasion and each one more breathtaking than the last. "I had this vague idea that if Sam was around it would prevent me from throwing you on the kitchen table and wildly ravishing you. I should have known that nothing goes the way I planned where you're concerned. The minute I walked through the door, I knew I was in trouble. My chaperone had deserted me, and my love was slightly naked and more than slightly tipsy. You'll notice that my self-control lasted a good sixteen or seventeen minutes."

"I noticed," Gabby said. "Quite the longest sixteen or seventeen minutes in my life. What would you have done if I hadn't come knocking on your door?"

He gave the question serious consideration while chewing on a section of grapefruit. "Remember, love, I was waiting for *you* to make the first move. I would have taken a cold shower, done a few rigorous calisthenics . . . probably killed another ten or twenty minutes before I battered down your door."

"I admire a man with self-control," Gabby said, gazing at him with all the sincerity her baby-blue eyes could muster. "Really I do. I just don't want you to think it's necessary to control your baser instincts on my account."

"For the next fifty-nine minutes," he said sternly, "I can handle it." He fixed Gabby with an intense look and slid his chair back several inches. "Keep your feet to yourself, madam. I'm trying to prove a point here. What do you want to do for the next hour?"

They stared at each other, nonplussed. "There's always the dishes," she muttered. "I doubt anyone could get amorous scrubbing egg yolk off Corningware." As she spoke, she noticed that Mike's eyes had drifted down to her breasts, and he seemed to have lost interest in the conversation. She followed his gaze, realizing two of the buttons on his blue shirt had given way, presumably from strain. "Oh, dear. Excuse me."

"The first thing on the agenda," he said, quite loudly, "is clothing. Lots of clothing. I know, we'll go for a walk on the beach and work up an appetite for lunch. How does that sound?"

"Tiring." Gabby slid her chair forward a bit and walked two fingers up his arm, eensy-weensy-spider style. "And cold. It's raining outside, if you haven't noticed. Now, I have a wonderful idea. How about making use of that fireplace in the bedroom? We could curl up on the rug and . . . work up an appetite for lunch."

He wavered, golden eyes darkening briefly with an intent, drowsy glow. "You, my love," he said thickly, "are developing a rug fetish." He cleared his throat and began stacking the dirty dishes on the table. "You dress and I'll take care of the egg yolk. And wear something that makes allowances for a bust measurement, will you?"

"It's *raining*," Gabby repeated, jabbing her index finger at the kitchen window for emphasis.

"All the better. Wear a raincoat, something nice and long and baggy. If you didn't bring anything suitable, I've got an old army poncho around here somewhere. Be ready in ten minutes and I'll give you a special treat."

"A bubble bath," Gabby suggested hopefully, "for two?"

"There are no sand crabs in a bubble bath," Mike said, a gleam of humor lighting his eyes. "And you, my tempting little witch, are going to learn how to catch sand crabs this morning."

"I can hardly wait," she murmured without enthusiasm, pinching him on a delectable terry-covered rear end as she passed.

Gabby discovered that walking the beach in a rainstorm was indeed an excellent way to work up an appetite. Trying to stay vertical when a stinging wind was determined to render you horizontal had to be good for a few thousand calories, at least. The salt spray was like fog, and steel-gray thunderclouds bubbled across the sky. A steady curtain of rain swept sideways along the beach, buffeting the jagged cliffs and sending spirals of rocks and sand into the sky. Judging from the lightning that flared occasionally along the horizon, the worst of the storm was yet to come.

Even covered with Mike's green army poncho, she was soaked to the skin within minutes. Her shoes grew one size with every step she took, coated with layer upon layer of wet sand and an occasional trailing bit of seaweed. The race to catch sand crabs was something she would write about in her diary and then try to forget for the remainder of her life. It involved waiting at the edge of the waterline until a wave washed the beach, then running like a demon to catch the crabs before they buried themselves in the sand. The really tricky part was spotting the air bubble in the sand that gave away the crab's hiding place, then unearthing it——she, he, whatever—before the next wave came and flattened you where you stood.

When Gabby was nearly washed out to sea on her second attempt, she said a nasty word and sat on a very wet rock until Mike had proved himself superior by catching sixteen sand crabs to her one. Then he let them go, which made the whole exercise rather pointless as far as Gabby was concerned. To pass the time while her lover was chasing crustaceans, she drew hearts in the sand with a soggy piece of driftwood. Mike loves Gabby, Gabrielle loves Michael, Michael William II loves Irish ... every combination she could think of had a two-minute lifespan until another wave came and swept the sand clean. Gabby was amazed that thoughts of love came so easily to her today, as if her surrender last night had broken down the last barrier between her and Mike. *She loved Michael Hyatt.* She could think it, write it, say it (but very softly, so as not to alarm him) without a single qualm. She was very careful not to think about the future, remembering how badly her previous relationships had ended when she had attempted any sort of commitment. Mike hadn't asked her for commitment. He had asked her to walk on the beach in a rainstorm and catch sand crabs and fix him a bacon and tomato sandwich for lunch. That much she could handle. A day at a time, a step at a time. No past, no future, no demands to be made or met. Mike had said it sounded like hell, but it felt like heaven to Gabby.

Once home, Mother Nature started clicking behind Mike's eyes. He leaned against the wall in the kitchen, watching Gabby struggle out of the wet poncho and the size fifty-three Adidas with the rapt attention men usually reserve for a striptease show. Gabby wiggled uneasily under his gaze, wondering what on earth he found so interesting. Her hair was plastered to her head like limp seaweed, and the wool cardigan she wore had taken on the distinct odor of wet sheep. Unlike the sparkling wet nymphets in the soft-drink commercials on television, she did not look good in water. She merely looked wet.

Mike, however, was another story altogether. Watching him surreptitiously beneath the towel that covered her wet head, Gabby decided that he looked almost as good in water as he did in sunlight, lamplight, and candlelight. His hair had darkened to a hundred shades of creamy brown, his supple skin appeared bronze, his eyes shimmered with watery sun. His clothes clung to the hard planes and angles she had memorized during the night. She ached with wanting.

"Time does fly when you're having fun," he murmured, consulting his watch. "Did you know it's already ten minutes after twelve?"

"Really?" Gabby said faintly. "Mike . . . what are you doing?"

"Taking off my shirt, of course." He advanced toward her, and the shirt fell to the floor with a wet slap. "It's foolish to stand around wearing wet clothes. You could get pneumonia. Do you need some help taking off that woolly thing of yours?"

"I can manage. Mike, if you think we're going to jump into bed just because your sixty minutes have passed . . ."

"Seventy minutes," he corrected softly. "Do you climb out of the top of that sweater, or out of the bottom?"

Gabby began retreating, feeling behind her for the swinging doors. "I'm warning you, Mike. I won't be dictated to by a watch."

He followed her into the hall. "You're just angry because I caught the most sand crabs. It's understandable."

"Did it ever occur to you that I might not be in the mood? You can't leave your pants there. You're going to ruin your carpet."

"Probably. I have a terrific idea. Let's make love in every room in the house. We can start right here in the living room. Jump up on the piano."

She made it to the landing at the top of the stairs before he caught her, swinging her up and over his shoulder as if she were a giant bag of potatoes. By the time she found her voice and ordered him to put her down, he already had—tossing her squarely in the middle of her bed.

"Joke," he said, though he didn't have much breath left from laughing. "Joke, sweetheart. No, don't squirm around like that, you're going to hurt yourself." He straddled her on the bed, pinning her flailing arms above her head. "What did you think I was going to do, jump your bones on the Steinway?"

"Michael William, when I get my hands on you—"

The threat was never completed. Still laughing, Mike closed her mouth with a kiss. Gabby struggled for a moment, but only until the atmosphere between them changed and the smile left his lips. She felt it drift away, along with his lighthearted mood. He lifted his head slowly, looking into her eyes with hypnotic intensity. Gabby lost pace with her breath, her teeth digging into her lower lip to still the trembling she couldn't control. Her face was flushed with emotion, and she wondered dazedly why her field of vision was sparkling with tears.

"I love you," he whispered. The tawny eyes were strained, as though the words were painfully inadequate. He touched his fingertips to the pink mist on her cheekbones, and only then did Gabby realize her hands were free.

"Mike?" Her shaking fingers framed his face, and she knew the raw emotions revealed in his eyes were reflected in hers. The aching need, the barely controlled desire, the faint whisper of fear . . . and the love.

The words didn't come easily to her. At first she told him with her body, twisting into him with a sudden fierce passion that annihilated gentleness and self-restraint. They shed clothing and inhibitions with trembling impatience, and only when Gabby was mindless and shivering, verging on the heights he had led her to, was she able to say it: "I love you, I love you . . ."

And then she was beyond rational thought, communicating only with her senses until violent shudders racked her slender body and her blood ran like scorching rain.

In the aftermath of love, his body intertwined with hers in a warm cocoon, Mike slept. Gabby held him in her arms and watched the rain drizzling down the window like fat, oily tears. She was satiated, her limbs heavy with fulfillment, yet she could not banish a chilling whisper of fear.

Outside the world was waiting.

"I want to have a picnic," Mike said.

They were preparing an early dinner: French bread and Brie, sliced roast beef and fresh fruit. Gabby glanced up from the strawberries she was hulling, pointing her paring knife in Mike's direction. "No. No and no again. I chased those nasty little crabs in the rain all morning. After two showers, I still have sand in places I have never had sand in before. As long as the high-wind warning is in effect, I am not setting foot out of this house."

"But it's my birthday."

"If you expect me to swallow that—"

He pulled his wallet out of the back pocket of his jeans, flipped it open to his driver's license, and dangled it under her nose. She read the birthdate printed below his name and her mouth dropped open. "Mike . . . it *is* your birthday."

He stole a strawberry and popped it into his mouth. "I'm aware of that. And I want a picnic."

"But why didn't you tell me? I don't have anything to give you."

He leaned one hip against the counter, a smile lurking in the compelling brown eyes. "How can you say that? What about our little bubble bath, hmm? And what about the musk oil you rubbed into—"

"Those weren't birthday presents," Gabby mumbled hastily, avoiding his eyes. "I meant *presents*, like shirts and ties and cologne."

"I can honestly say that I enjoyed the musk oil far more than—"

The telephone rang, cutting short his erotic trip down memory lane. He winked at Gabby as he moved to answer it, grinning at the faint color suffusing her face. "Hello? . . . Oh, Gina . . . thank you. No, I'm not forty years old, brat. I'm thirty-five, as you very well know."

Gabby put down the knife and wiped her hands on a paper towel. Gina. Gina who knew it was his birthday, Gina whom Mike was obviously fond of, judging by the tone of his voice. She turned on the water in the sink in an unsuccessful attempt to drown out the conversation.

"No, I'm staying here. No, with a friend . . . yes, she is. No, you *can't*. It's a private party. I've got to go. Tell Jenny and Heidi hello for me."

Gabby's head swiveled and she stared at him in wide-eyed amazement. Gina, Jenny, Heidi? Mike smiled and blew her a kiss.

"Yes, Gina . . . I promise. No, I don't know, Nosey. Yes, I *promise*. Bye." He hung up the receiver and stifled a sigh. "Sisters. The plague of my life."

"Oh." Gabby let out the breath she had been holding and began wiping off the counter. The strawberries had stained the Formica, and she scrubbed until her arm ached. "How many do you have?" she asked casually.

"Sisters? Too many. Five at the last count, and four of them are married with little plagues of their own. What about you?"

Gabby scrubbed harder. "What about me? Mike, do

you have any Comet or Ajax?"

"Under the sink," he said. "Do you have any sisters or brothers?"

Gabby felt a cold hard knot braiding and unbraiding in her stomach. She found the Ajax and shook a small mountain of it on the drain before she answered. "No. I was adopted. Aunt Helen didn't have any other children."

"Irish, you're going to scrub the Formica off. Here." He took the Ajax and the dishrag out of her hands and pushed her toward the table. "Sit. While I get ready for our picnic, you're going to tell me about Aunt Helen."

"I might tell you about Aunt Helen," Gabby said mutinously, "but you are not dragging me out on that beach again for a picnic, birthday or no."

"Did I say we were going to picnic on the beach? Then stop jumping to conclusions and tell me about your aunt."

While Mike filled a straw hamper he produced from the pantry, Gabby quietly began to talk. She deliberately avoided any mention of dates that might raise questions in his mind, proceeding as if she had been born at the age of nine when Helen Andrews had first taken her out of the Catholic girls' home. There was no lacerating inner struggle over whether she should confide the truth to Mike. The devastating meeting with Mrs. DeSpain was still too fresh, burning like an acid spill in her brain. Although common sense told her that the man she loved would never react in the same way, she wasn't prepared to take the chance.

She concentrated instead on the strong-willed school-teacher who had managed to give her a normal life in less than normal circumstances. She described her in detail, the whimsical features, the sparkling hazel eyes, the booming, Ethel Merman-type voice so at odds with the fragile appearance. She smiled as she remembered her aunt tumbling head over heels in love at the unlikely age of sixty-seven. She had done it as she had done everything in her life, with such wholehearted enthusiasm that more than once Gabby had found herself waiting up in the wee hours of the morning, one eye on the clock and the other on the front door.

She talked, carefully remembering the good times, only the good times. She talked until she realized that Mike was seated across the table from her and had been for some time, and the picnic hamper was neatly packed, waiting on the kitchen counter.

"I'm sorry," she apologized with a nervous little laugh. "I didn't mean to talk your ear off. Now I've bored you with my entire life story."

"Hardly. As a matter of fact, when I was talking to my sister, I realized how little I really know about you. She asked me how old you were, and I couldn't even tell her that. You keep a very low profile, my love. How old *are* you, anyway? We may have to end this whole relationship here and now if I discover I'm robbing the cradle."

"Twenty-seven." Gabby smiled. "I'll be twenty-eight in December. I have all my own teeth and I'm allergic to penicillin."

"I can live with that. I'll have to call my sister and put her mind at ease. She's probably tearing her hair out, imagining I'm holed up in here with some underage Lolita. Gina is the maternal type who always needs a cause. As long as I can remember"—he grimaced—"I've been it. All right, now it's your turn."

"To do what?"

"Ask questions. You're probably the least inquisitive woman I've ever met in my life. Isn't there something you're dying to know about me? Credit references, childhood diseases, police record?"

She stared at him, wide-eyed. "You don't, do you? Have a police record?"

"Of course not. But how would you have known if you hadn't asked?"

"You have a point," she returned dryly. "All right, here's one: Do you really make paper clips for a living?"

"Yes," he said promptly. "Also steel plates, tubing, and other miscellaneous items."

"Oh. Do you own your own company?"

"Yes. Hyatt Steel Corporation. My father founded it, but he retired several years ago. Thank heaven, none of my sisters wanted to come into the business, or I would have joined the army."

"Do you like musk oil?"

As a diversion from families and past history, it worked very well. The half-playful light in his eyes faded as he looked at her, and she heard the quick catch of his breath. "I do now," he said softly. For a long moment, hazy passion softened his features. Then he shook his head faintly and stood, pulling Gabby to her feet. "Come, my love. You have just been invited to my private birthday party. It's semi-formal—did I tell you?"

Gabby glanced down at her open-weave smock and

strawberry-stained jeans. Entering into the spirit of the festivities, she said brightly, "How much time do I have?"

"Fifteen minutes," he responded. "Not a second more. I'll call for you at your door."

"Mike, if I put on a nice dress and you take me out in that hurricane—"

"Fie on you, woman!" He sent her out of the kitchen with a slap on her bottom. "Fourteen minutes and counting. Move it!"

She changed into a floor-length dress of white cotton and lace. It had been designed with a wide eyelet ruffle that could be worn either on or off the shoulders. Gabby adjusted it modestly on her shoulders, then reminded herself it was Mike's birthday and tugged it down, revealing the dusky shadow between her breasts. She left her hair free, parted in the center to softly frame her face. A quick reapplication of makeup and she was ready, at the exact moment a light tap sounded at the bedroom door. She took one last glance in the mirror, barely recognizing this new image of herself. Her eyes had a liquid sheen, delicately tinged with blue shadows; her lips were soft and faintly swollen. She wore Mike's love like a living, breathing thing, and it added a dimension of beauty she had never seen in herself before.

There was a moment of silence when she opened the door. He had changed into a dress shirt and slacks—her peripheral vision confirmed this while her gaze never left his face. His eyes seemed to take in everything about her, from the sudden uncertainty in her stance to the tiny pearl studs she wore in her ears. He lifted his hand, gently tracing a faint, finger-shaped bruise beneath her collarbone. "Did I do that?" he asked huskily.

"The bubble bath," Gabby said absently, closing her eyes and savoring the simple touch that sensitized every fiber and nerve ending in her body. "Remember when you and I—"

"I'd better not," he whispered, pressing an apologetic kiss on the bruised flesh. "If I do, you'll never see my surprise." He spared a brief, wistful glance at Gabby's bed, then set his shoulders and took her hand in his. "Your picnic awaits, my lady."

He took her up a narrow flight of stairs to his attic, an attic unlike any other Gabby had seen. It ran the entire length of the house, a secret, tunnel-shaped room with a parade of stained-glass skylights and a magnificent view of the storm raging overhead. On a clear summer day, Gabby imagined the room would be stifling with rising heat, washed from end to end with the hot yellow and orange hues of the diamond-shaped skylights. But now, when the sunset was lost in slate-gray clouds and the sounds of rain went on and on above their heads . . . now the attic was magical.

Mike had set the scene for his very private birthday picnic. He had spread a soft patchwork quilt of variegated blues and white on the varnished floorboards. The hamper he had packed rested in the center of the quilt, as did a smoky bottle of wine and two long-stemmed glasses. Candles in wrought-iron holders flickered from the floor around the quilt and atop the shadowy furniture stored along the walls.

"Happy birthday to me," Mike murmured, lifting her hair and kissing the delicate curve of her neck. "Better than the beach?"

"Better." Her voice was high and thin, a whisper of sound. She was lost in love, dazzled by this extraordinary man who never ceased to surprise her. Candles. Laughter. Passion that lingered beneath the hum-drum business of life. How had she survived before loving someone became more than an elusive dream? In that instant, she felt deeply and sincerely sorry for anyone in the world who was not Gabrielle Cates. Lordy, what they were missing.

They sat cross-legged on the quilt, facing each other over a dripping candle that smelled of jasmine. After two glasses of wine—a liquid appetizer, according to her host—Gabby very properly sang "Happy Birthday" to Mike, then proceeded to feed him strawberries that had been dipped in milk chocolate. She barely noticed the rain that flowed like a river over the skylights, hardly blinked when the occasional flash of lightning brought a noon-day brightness to the room. They were in the eye of the hurricane, safe and inviolate from the elements beyond.

Candlelight added a luminous texture to the air around them. Gabby was entranced by the soft pastel shadings on Mike's features, by the slow light that filled his eyes when she touched the rim of the wineglass to her lips. The heat from the guttering candles brought a moist sheen to her skin and a sensual, slow-motion lassitude to her movements. She was warm and growing warmer from the inside out. She abandoned conversation to drink in the picture Mike made, leaning with unconscious grace over the smoking candle, one finger idly slicing through the blue-white flame. Then their eyes met and he took the wineglass from her unresisting fingers, setting it carefully to the side. They came together over jasmine smoke at an unhurried pace, eyes clinging, backs arching. He drank the wine from her lips, no other parts of their bodies touching. When he lifted his head to look at her, there was a smoldering urgency beneath the gentle question. Gabby answered with a smile, then pursed her lips and blew the candle out between them.

Mike stood in one fluid movement, pinching the candlewicks out until only one remained. He placed the wrought-iron holder in her hands, then picked her up in his arms with a gentle reminder not to set his shirt on fire. He carried her down the flickering stairwell, through the bright blaze of the hallway and into the purple shadows of his bedroom. Still in his arms, Gabby had just set the candle on his dresser when a blinding flash of light exploded around them, followed almost immediately by a deafening clap of thunder that literally shook the walls of the house. Gabby buried her face against Mike's shirt, covering her ringing eardrums with her palms. When she opened her eyes again, the house was trembling in darkness. Even the candle on the dresser had gone out, gasping in a wispy spiral.

"It's fate," she whispered unsteadily, clinging to Mike's shoulders as he lowered her to the ground. "I'm destined to go through the rest of my life in total darkness."

"I want you to stay here." He moved over to the smoking candle, lighting it quickly with a book of matches produced from his pocket. "I'll need to take this with me, but I'll be right back."

Gabby trailed after him to the door, stubbing her toe on the corner of a bookcase. "Ouch! Mike, wait . . . can't

I go with you? I don't want to be left alone here."

"Not until I know it's safe. If that lightning didn't hit the house, it came damn close. This is perfect country for a brush fire. *Now stay here.*"

She did as she was told, less out of obedience than because of the simple fact that she couldn't see to follow him. He was gone long enough for her to chew several nails off, not quite long enough for her to work up the courage to stumble back to the attic for another candle. When he returned, his clothes were drenched and he had exchanged the candle for a battery-operated lantern. He barely glanced at her, moving to the closet and pulling out a light-colored windbreaker. "It struck a power line," he said brusquely. "There's a live wire across the road."

Gabby watched helplessly as he shrugged into the jacket. "Where are you going?"

"I have to drive into town and find a phone. The lines are dead downstairs."

Gabby stood rock-still in the center of the room, her eyes following him as he fumbled on the dresser for his car keys. There was something vaguely, hauntingly familiar about the cold fist of dread that curled her stomach. "Mike . . . don't go. Wait until tomorrow, wait until the storm lets up."

"Gabby, there are five thousand volts of electricity dancing across the highway. I have to report it so they can get a repair crew out here." He thrust the lantern into her hand, and her frozen fingers clamped automatically around the metal handle. "I won't be long, sixty minutes at the outside."

"Take me with you." Her voice was thin, colorless.

"There's no need for you to go out in this mess, Irish. It's my birthday; you have to do what I say." Cold lips pressed briefly against her forehead. "Keep the bed warm for me. I'll be back before you know it."

Minutes later, she heard the powerful motor of the Porsche humming. She went to the window and watched until the twin beams of light disappeared in the storm.

And suddenly a flashback of another time echoed through her mind, another farewell, another cold sheet of glass beneath her palms. The memory hit her with the impact of a physical blow.

I'll be back before you know it.

Vision blurred. Gabby backed across the room through an arc of white lightning, her eyes fixed unblinkingly on the window.

I'll be back before you know it.

The words, her mother's words, whirled in circles through Gabby's mind, gaining in momentum until a low scream gathered and burned in her throat. She wanted to run and stop him, but it was too late. Long before she had ever loved him, it had been too late.

Dear God. She had been so blissfully happy, basking in her newfound ability to *truly* love. And like a child taking his first tottering steps, she had never paused to consider the possibility of a nasty fall. She had never stopped to remember the pain that loving could bring.

Until now.

Chapter

10

THE NIGHTMARE CAME true, just as she knew it would.

Gabby waited helplessly, and for the first time in so many years, there was no inner sanctuary in which to take refuge from the pain. She waited in the dark, sitting on Mike's bed. When the promised hour turned into two, she took the lantern downstairs and waited on the couch. She was still waiting when the hard rain stopped falling and the skies lightened with a watery dawn.

Mike had been gone nearly five hours.

She tried the telephone throughout the long night, finally getting a dial tone. Fingers trembling, she called the closest hospital in the area. As far as she could discover, there had been no accidents reported during the night. She had her hand on the receiver to call the police when the telephone rang.

"Gabby?" It was the first time she had heard Mike's voice on the phone. He sounded tired, and very far away. "I've been trying to get you all night, love. The lines were all down until just now."

"Are you all right?" Relief and anguish colored her voice in equal measure. He was alive, he was well. Now there were no more excuses to postpone the inevitable.

Static. ". . . on the road. It's still blocked."

"What? We've got a bad connection."

"There was a mudslide about six miles west of the beachhouse. I couldn't get back. They say the road should be clear within an hour. Are you okay?"

"Fine." An hour. More than enough time for her to make her getaway. Now that she knew what she must do, providence seemed to be providing every opportunity. There would be no painful good-byes, another gift from a suddenly sympathetic fate.

"I'll be home soon. We'll have to have a belated birthday party." More static. "Did you hear me?"

"No."

"I said I love you."

Gabby's eyes felt bruised with the effort of holding back the tears. "I love you, too." And then, hoarsely, "I'm sorry, Mike. Please forgive me."

Hands shaking, she replaced the receiver. It rang again almost immediately, but she was already halfway up the stairs. It rang at intervals while she was packing her clothes, rang again when sheer nerves had her doubled over and violently ill in the bathroom. She changed her stained cotton dress for jeans and a sweater, filled her arms with her few pieces of luggage and walked out to her car. She took in several deep breaths of the rain-washed air, but she couldn't seem to get much oxygen. She noticed a bright orange repair truck pulled over to the sandy shoulder of the highway, emergency lights flashing. A snakelike coil dropped from a nearby powerline to the road, flashing and sparking like some sort of malfunctioning firecracker. If the repair crew could get through the mudslide area, obviously Mike could, too. There was no time to waste.

The black Porsche would be coming from the west. Gabby turned east, driving into the sunrise. Mike would never forgive her for leaving him like this. She hoped he would hate her. *Zack and Alan . . . and Mike makes three . . .*

He would automatically assume she had once again run away from commitment, from her own inability to care deeply for anyone else. He would never realize she had left because she cared too much, because she had had a brief glimpse of what losing him could do to her, because she had to leave while she could still survive alone. It had taken him such a short time to slip beneath her guard, to break down the walls she had built up around her emotions. How much time would it have taken before he had become indispensable to her, before he had the power to destroy her?

Her subconscious knew where she was going long before she knew it herself. She drove along the coast for several hours, stopping only once for gas and a cup of coffee. Then she turned inland, following a gravel road that continually switched back on itself high into the mountains. The terrain grew rugged and densely wooded. Gabby felt nothing but a crushing fatigue, and she rolled down her window so the cool mountain air would keep her alert. There were no tears, just as there were no words in her mind.

It seemed as if she blinked, and suddenly she was there. Nothing felt familiar, yet she recognized the few ghostlike remains of the tiny California mill town where she had been born. A gas station, boarded up at the windows and overgrown with weeds. Pierce's Body Shop, a hollow plaster shell with obscene graffiti spray-painted on the walls. The post office and the drugstore, also boarded up.

As if her subconscious had been working on it all along, the answer flashed into her mind. She had come back to concede, to acknowledge the victory of a past that would never die. In the end, even her love for Mike had not been as strong as her deep-rooted fears. She couldn't escape the past. It was impossible. It always would be.

She didn't drive straight to the house. She lost her way twice, the Rabbit kicking up clouds of dust on the side roads that crisscrossed the mountain. Eventually, she found the right turnoff, a lonely country lane walled with straggling chokecherry bushes. When she pulled up in front of the small, wood-sided house, she stared at it in vague surprise. The distorted memories of childhood had left an impression of a dark and forbidding home, possessing an almost haunted atmosphere. This tiny frame building merely looked empty. The front door was hanging by one hinge; the windows were broken or missing. The awning over the front porch had collapsed, leaning drunkenly to one side. A squirrel chattered shrilly from the roof.

Gabby sat in the car, waiting for the expected flood of bitterness and rejection. Nothing. After several minutes, she pushed open the door and climbed out into the bright sunshine. She stretched stiff limbs in the heat, then walked slowly around the dusty hood of the car and up the rotting front steps. It was like an obstacle course, ducking beneath the precarious tilt of the awning, stepping over missing planks in the porch, slipping sideways through the front door that creaked gently in the breeze.

The house was dark and cool, stripped clean of everything with the exception of the metal kitchen cabinets. Gabby walked through empty doorways from room to room. She looked through a battered screen door at the overgrown backyard where she had once played. She stood before the living-room window, in the exact same spot she had stood once before.

Nothing.

She squinted into the sunlight, breathing the fresh mountain air through the broken glass. She was aware of an emotion flowing through her body from the tips of her toes to the nerve centers of her brain, an emotion she couldn't immediately put a name to. She waited while the sensation grew stronger, as if fed by a bubbling underground spring.

She felt free.

There were no ghosts here. There were memories, but they no longer had the power to hurt her. She had not been responsible for her mother's actions. With a startling, unfamiliar rush of identity, of *pride,* she realized that she had not been the victim, after all. Her mother had been the real loser, and finally Gabby pitied her. She heard the words echo in her mind one last time: *I'll be back before you know it,* and she saw the lie in her mother's face, but this time she forgave her.

Mike. How many of the brand-new qualities she suddenly recognized in herself had she first seen through his eyes? He loved her, and his love had *not* made her more vulnerable as she had once feared. It had made her stronger. Love was more than the power to hurt someone. It was also the power to heal.

She whirled from the window and out of the house, taking the front steps in one flying leap. The hell with caution, fear, always holding back, protecting herself. Never again. Her life began today, now, from this moment on. And, in spite of everything, she was going to be just fine.

His car was parked in the driveway. The Porsche looked as if it had had a very rough night. It had been humbled with a layer of dust and grime, and the ornate silver hubcaps were thick with dried mud. It looked almost compatible side by side with her travel-weary Rabbit.

The security gates were open, the alarm system turned off. Gabby searched the house from top to bottom, including the attic, where stale food rested on a patchwork quilt. No Mike. The only evidence that his incredible car had not driven itself home was a dirty coffee cup in the kitchen sink.

Outside again. She ran through the garden, fragrant with the damp essence of spring rain, down the terraced steps that led to the beach. Quite possibly the most beautiful rainbow-hued sunset that had ever graced southern California was smeared over the ocean. Later, Gabby was only to remember that it had definitely stopped raining and the sky was a nice pink. Her mind was elsewhere.

He was sitting alone on the water-packed sand, barefoot, gazing toward the wind-ruffled ocean. His profile was pure, clean of expression, his tawny eyes dark and hooded. His too long, light-rinsed hair lifted and swirled with the breeze. A movement in his lap caught Gabby's eye as she approached, and she discovered that he was not alone after all. Kitty arched and stretched under the absent, rhythmic strokes of his hand. Had Gabby found a sea turtle sitting in his lap, she couldn't have been more astonished.

She knew the exact moment when he became aware of her presence. He never so much as blinked, and his hand continued with the Kitty massage, but Gabby felt the entire scope of his awareness zeroing in on her.

She dug her hands in the pockets of her jeans and said quietly, "Did I miss the party?"

"No." One finger tickled Kitty's ears, breast, stomach. He rolled over and purred in ecstasy, which was understandable. "We were waiting for you to show up."

A pause. "Have you been waiting long?"

"All my life." No sooner were the words out of his mouth than his hand snaked out and caught the closest thing to him—which happened to be her ankle. A quick flip of his wrist and Gabby tumbled into his arms. Kitty escaped being a third party in the embrace with a snarl and a sideways lunge, but Gabby had no such inclination. She went down to Mike like hot wax, returning his ruthless kisses with a hungry desperation of her own. She couldn't give enough. Her love was open and flowing, and as real and tangible as their two bodies straining together. This was the stuff that life was made of, this miracle, this truth.

He withdrew from her, breathing hard, gazing into her face as if he could never get enough of her. His cheek was coated with sand, and the hands that cradled her face were cold and gritty. He was beautiful. "I figured it this way," he said. "You *had* to come back. I loved you too much to even consider anything else."

"Besides"—Gabby feathered sandy kisses along his jaw—"I forgot my cat. Thank you for taking such good care of him."

"Don't misunderstand. I still don't like him."

"You were petting him."

His smile was a miracle of solar energy. "You're home now. I can pet you."

Home. The use of the word turned Gabby's eyes to blue mist. "Mike," she said softly. "I want you, Mike."

"I hope so," he breathed unsteadily, "because I'm all yours, Irish."

"I love you," Gabby whispered, gazing into liquid-gold eyes. "I love you so very much."

"This seems like an excellent time," he said hesitantly, "to make a few confessions."

"You love cats," Gabby said, and was promptly and thoroughly kissed.

"No chance. I told you I hated cats, which was true. I also told you I was a confirmed bachelor, which was strategy."

"Strategy," Gabby echoed, dutifully attentive.

"Strategy. Do you remember the first time I saw you?"

"How could I forget?" Gabby muttered. "My wedding day."

"No." There was an uncertain pause. "Actually, it was the night before. I saw you from my balcony. You were wearing a wet football jersey and feeding seagulls. I took one look at you and decided I'd found my one and only. You can't imagine how lousy I felt when I saw you walk out of the house the next morning in that wedding dress."

"You saw me?" Gabby frowned. "When? How?"

"I was down on the beach trying to figure out how to meet you. I had a perfect view of the bride leaving for the church. So I did what any normal depressed man would do."

"Oh, dear." Gabby pressed her cheek against his chest. "You got drunk. You got drunk, and that night—"

"That night I stumbled over a runaway bride and her cat on the beach. The rest you know . . . except for Samantha."

"Samantha," Gabby said weakly. "I think you'd better kiss me before you tell me any more surprises."

His mouth searched for and found hers, and it was several minutes before he said thickly, "She's my sister."

Gabby's thumb dragged slowly across the moistness of his bottom lip. "Who?"

"Samantha. She's my sister, the youngest and the only one still unattached. When you lost the lease on your cottage, I had to do some creative thinking to keep you within arm's reach. I arranged to buy the cottage from Paulsen—"

"You *what?*"

"I bought the damn cottage," he repeated, flushing beneath his tan. "Also being aware of your financial situation, I convinced Samantha—she *is* an actress, by the way—to pretend to be Paulsen's new tenant. A stroke," he added smugly, "of genius. She flushed her best angora sweater down the toilet just to bring us closer together."

"She flushed . . . you mean, when the cottage flooded . . . I'll *kill* her."

"At the wedding," Mike said. "She'll be there with bells on. She said to tell you."

Gabby's mouth was still open when a wave nudged their legs, soaking through already soaking jeans. Gabby scooped up a damp cat and they struggled to their feet in the sand. She looked at the foam-flecked water surrounding them with a powerful sense of déjà-vu. She had so many things to tell Mike, so many things to explain. But it would have to wait.

Mike took the cat out of her hands and gestured grandly to the cliff behind them. "After you, my lady."

Holding on to each other and an angry cat, it was difficult to keep their balance. But they managed.

SECOND CHANCE AT LOVE

COMING NEXT MONTH
IN THE
SECOND CHANCE AT LOVE SERIES

SECOND CHANCE AT LOVE

Be Sure to Read These New Releases!

HEARTS ARE WILD #298 by Janet Gray
High-stakes poker player Emily Farrell never
loses her cool and *never* gambles on love—until alluring
Michael Mategna rips away her aloof façade and exposes
her soft, womanly yearnings.

SPRING MADNESS #299 by Aimée Duvall
The airwaves sizzle when zany deejay Meg
Randall and steamy station owner Kyle Rager join
forces to beat the competition...and end up
madly wooing each other.

SIREN'S SONG #300 by Linda Barlow
Is Cat MacFarlane a simple singer or a criminal
accomplice? Is Rob Hepburn a UFO investigator or
the roguish descendant of a Scots warrior clan? Their
suspicions entangle them in intrigue...and passion!

MAN OF HER DREAMS #301 by Katherine Granger
Jessie Dillon's looking for her one true love—and
she's sure Jake McGuire isn't it! How can a devious
scoundrel in purple sneakers who inspires such
toe-tingling lust possibly be the man of her dreams?

UNSPOKEN LONGINGS #302 by Dana Daniels
Joel Easterwood is a friend when Lesley Evans
needs one most. But she's secretly loved him since
childhood, and his intimate ministrations are
tearing her apart!

THIS SHINING HOUR #303 by Antonia Tyler
Kent Sawyer's blindness hasn't diminished his
amazing self-reliance...or breathtaking sexual appeal.
But is Eden Fairchild brave enough to allow this
extraordinary man to care for *her*?

Order on opposite page

SECOND CHANCE AT LOVE

___ 0-425-08285-7	**NIGHT OF A THOUSAND STARS #275** Petra Diamond	$2.25
___ 0-425-08286-5	**UNDERCOVER KISSES #276** Laine Allen	$2.25
___ 0-425-08287-3	**MAN TROUBLE #277** Elizabeth Henry	$2.25
___ 0-425-08288-1	**SUDDENLY THAT SUMMER #278** Jennifer Rose	$2.25
___ 0-425-08289-X	**SWEET ENCHANTMENT #279** Diana Mars	$2.25
___ 0-425-08461-2	**SUCH ROUGH SPLENDOR #280** Cinda Richards	$2.25
___ 0-425-08462-0	**WINDFLAME #281** Sarah Crewe	$2.25
___ 0-425-08463-9	**STORM AND STARLIGHT #282** Lauren Fox	$2.25
___ 0-425-08464-7	**HEART OF THE HUNTER #283** Liz Grady	$2.25
___ 0-425-08465-5	**LUCKY'S WOMAN #284** Delaney Devers	$2.25
___ 0-425-08466-3	**PORTRAIT OF A LADY #285** Elizabeth N. Kary	$2.25
___ 0-425-08508-2	**ANYTHING GOES #286** Diana Morgan	$2.25
___ 0-425-08509-0	**SOPHISTICATED LADY #287** Elissa Curry	$2.25
___ 0-425-08510-4	**THE PHOENIX HEART #288** Betsy Osborne	$2.25
___ 0-425-08511-2	**FALLEN ANGEL #289** Carole Buck	$2.25
___ 0-425-08512-0	**THE SWEETHEART TRUST #290** Hilary Cole	$2.25
___ 0-425-08513-9	**DEAR HEART #291** Lee Williams	$2.25
___ 0-425-08514-7	**SUNLIGHT AND SILVER #292** Kelly Adams	$2.25
___ 0-425-08515-5	**PINK SATIN #293** Jeanne Grant	$2.25
___ 0-425-08516-3	**FORBIDDEN DREAM #294** Karen Keast	$2.25
___ 0-425-08517-1	**LOVE WITH A PROPER STRANGER #295** Christa Merlin	$2.25
___ 0-425-08518-X	**FORTUNE'S DARLING #296** Frances Davies	$2.25
___ 0-425-08519-8	**LUCKY IN LOVE #297** Jacqueline Topaz	$2.25
___ 0-425-08626-7	**HEARTS ARE WILD #298** Janet Gray	$2.25
___ 0-425-08627-5	**SPRING MADNESS #299** Aimée Duvall	$2.25
___ 0-425-08628-3	**SIREN'S SONG #300** Linda Barlow	$2.25
___ 0-425-08629-1	**MAN OF HER DREAMS #301** Katherine Granger	$2.25
___ 0-425-08630-5	**UNSPOKEN LONGINGS #302** Dana Daniels	$2.25
___ 0-425-08631-3	**THIS SHINING HOUR #303** Antonia Tyler	$2.25
___ 0-425-08672-0	**THE FIRE WITHIN #304** Laine Allen	$2.25
___ 0-425-08673-9	**WHISPERS OF AN AUTUMN DAY #305** Lee Williams	$2.25
___ 0-425-08674-7	**SHADY LADY #306** Jan Mathews	$2.25
___ 0-425-08675-5	**TENDER IS THE NIGHT #307** Helen Carter	$2.25
___ 0-425-08676-3	**FOR LOVE OF MIKE #308** Courtney Ryan	$2.25
___ 0-425-08677-1	**TWO IN A HUDDLE #309** Diana Morgan	$2.25

Prices may be slightly higher in Canada.

Available at your local bookstore or return this form to:

SECOND CHANCE AT LOVE
Book Mailing Service
P.O. Box 690, Rockville Centre, NY 11571

Please send me the titles checked above. I enclose _____ Include 75¢ for postage and handling if one book is ordered; 25¢ per book for two or more not to exceed $1.75. California, Illinois, New York and Tennessee residents please add sales tax.

NAME _____

ADDRESS _____

CITY _____ STATE/ZIP _____

(allow six weeks for delivery)   **SK-41b**

A STIRRING PAGEANTRY
OF
HISTORICAL ROMANCE

❋❋❋❋❋

Shana Carrol

___ 0-515-08249-X Rebels in Love $3.95

Roberta Gellis

___ 0-515-08230-9 Bond of Blood $3.95

___ 0-515-07529-9 Fire Song $3.95

___ 0-425-07627-X A Tapestry of Dreams $6.95
                   (A Berkley Trade Paperback)

Ellen Tanner Marsh

___ 0-425-06536-7 Reap the Savage Wind $3.95

___ 0-425-07188-X Wrap Me in Splendor $3.95

Jill Gregory

___ 0-515-07100-5 The Wayward Heart $3.50

___ 0-515-07728-3 To Distant Shores $3.50

___ 0-425-07666-0 My True and Tender Love $6.95
                   (A Berkley Trade Paperback)

Mary Pershall

___ 0-425-07020-4 A Shield of Roses $3.95

Francine Rivers

___ 0-515-08181-7 Sycamore Hill $3.50

___ 0-515-06823-3 This Golden Valley $3.50

Pamela Belle

___ 0-425-08268-7 The Moon in the Water $3.95

___ 0-425-07367-X The Chains of Fate $6.95
                   (A Berkley Trade Paperback)

Prices may be slightly higher in Canada.